COCKTAIL

LAUREN SMITH

1

LONG ISLAND ICED TEA

"I'm the queen of bad dates," Aubree Cole muttered as she stood to watch her date walk out the front door of Love Potion #9, Chicago's trendiest new bar. He was already digging into the back pocket of those fine jeans; she knew what was coming before she heard the ping from her phone. Lifting it off the table, she saw the notification from the dating app Meet Cute. She read the message with dread.

LongIsland23 says: had a nice time but I don't think we're a fit.

Aubree slumped back into the booth and replayed the date from start to finish. All the awkward pauses rather than pleasant silences, the enthusiasm she'd had to be on a date and his apparent apprehension over her excitement. Had she seemed too eager? Too pathetic?

Through the windows, she could see the streets full of snow with people bundled up as they walked past. By contrast, the bar was warm, and popular music—the kind she liked, came in through the speakers overhead but not too loud. Despite the bar's welcoming atmosphere, Aubree couldn't help but feel detached from the outside world and even from the people in the room. She couldn't seem to manage a human connection in a romantic way. Dating hadn't been this hard in high school or college.

She glanced at her watch. It was only 9 o'clock, but she didn't have the strength to walk the one block to her apartment just yet. She'd really hoped *LongIsland23* would've been *the One*.

He had been charming and sexy in their messages. He joked about his dog and dropped innuendos in a way that left her anticipating each message. She'd been so excited to see him in the flesh and to touch that flesh. In person, he'd been every bit the investment banker stereotype: cold and stiff.

Pulling the app up again, she unmatched her profile from his and almost hit the button to start swiping again but stopped herself. What was the point? She had twelve bad dates in a row; there was no Mr. Perfect in sight. She felt like she was at the end of her rope when it came to dating. She glanced out the window again. Couples walked past hand in hand. It all seemed so easy, but she knew love and romance were anything but easy.

God, that stuff shouldn't matter. She was a liberated, independent woman of thirty-three with a fantastic job at the Chicago Board of Trade as the director of equities. She was fine. She had a nice apartment and a healthy 401k. She didn't *need* Mr. Perfect. But something was missing in her life. All of her friends were married with the whole 2.5 kids thing. Aubree had put so much effort into her career that until last year, she hadn't stopped working long enough to realize that she was lonely.

One night, after half a bottle of Pinot Grigio, she had let her best friend Amanda talk her into signing up for a dating app called Meet Cute. For a few days, she hadn't bothered to actually attempt matching with anyone. One weekend she was shopping and ran into an old college boyfriend, one who'd never dated a woman more than a month before dumping them. He'd been in a department store with his wife and two kids—a picture-perfect family. How Mr. Can't Settle Down had gotten married while she was still single had sent her straight back to the Meet Cute app. Since then, her dating life had gone from nonexistent to a train wreck.

She stared at the long island iced tea she'd ordered because she thought it would be cute given her date's screen name. The guy hadn't even cracked a smile when she explained her drink choice nor had he stuck around long enough to pay for his drink.

With a heavy sigh, Aubree called it a night. If she got home in time, she could watch one of those good thriller movies she'd been meaning to watch forever. She picked up her purse and headed toward the bar to settle her tab.

She glanced around and set her clutch down on the cherry wood bar top. The bar was empty. She leaned forward and peered over the edge of the bar to see if there might be a bartender crouched down to grab extra glasses or something. Aubree was still propped up over the counter, her elbows braced on the wood as the door at the end of one wall behind the bar swung open and a man stepped out behind the bar.

She couldn't help but stare at him. The man was gorgeous. Okay, way beyond gorgeous. He had broad shoulders and wore a light blue button up shirt with the cuffs rolled up to his elbows, exposing sun-tanned muscled skin. His trim waist accented by dark blue jeans that fit like a glove. Aubree's mouth ran dry as her gaze traveled up his body to his face.

He looked like Chris Hemsworth with a chiseled face that held a hint of delicious edginess. She usually fell for men who had that sweet, cute sort of boy-next-door look. But this guy? He was the boy next door who had aged a decade and then joined the Marines. A lock of dark blonde hair fell into his blue eyes; it was a little long, just enough that he could casually run his fingers through it. She noticed his mouth and those full lips that were moving as he stood in front of her. Then those lips stopped moving and he stared at her expectantly.

"Huh?" She suddenly blurted as she realized with complete and total mortification that the man had been talking to her.

"Another Long Island iced tea?" he asked in the most gorgeous Australian accent.

"Oh... no. Thanks." She blushed. "I just need to settle the tab for our table."

"Sure, hang on." He retrieved a black tablet and ran her table number. "Two drinks?"

"Yeah... My date had to leave early so—"

"So, he made you pay?" A look of open disgust crossed the man's face before he masked it with politeness.

"Yeah... Guess that should've been a tipoff that he wasn't the one." She retrieved her card and slid it over the lacquered bar surface toward him. The man took the card to process her payment. When he gave her the receipt, she saw only one drink on the tab.

"I had two drinks," she reminded him.

The bartender's lips twitched. "No woman in this bar is going to pay for a man's drink after being ditched on a date."

Aubree winced. "You saw him ditch me, huh?" She wanted to die right there. Everyone nearby must have seen her crash and burn on her date.

"I saw that asshole leave. So yeah, you don't pay for him."

"Thanks." She could afford to pay for the extra drink, but she appreciated the gesture.

"You want to talk about it?" The man pulled out a glass and set it down before her, but when she started to reach for her wallet again, he smiled.

"No worries. This one's on the house." He passed her a glass of something after he mixed it.

"What is it?" She eyed the brightly colored magenta flower he'd dropped in the top of the clear drink.

He leaned forward with his hands on the bar and his strong forearms showing thick, well defined muscles. That same lock of dark blond hair fell into his eyes again as he tipped his head toward her and lifted an eyebrow as he flashed her a conspiratorial smile that sent her stomach dancing with butterflies.

"Valley of the flowers. Snow leopard vodka, Mizu Shochu, and a couple of dashes of grapefruit bitters."

"Snow leopard vodka?" She took a sip as he watched her. His intense stare made her blush.

"Rare, like a good woman," he replied and then he left her alone to enjoy the drink. He filled half a dozen other orders while she sipped her cocktail. As he worked, she had a chance to spy on him. He smiled and laughed easily with the customers as he prepared drinks.

I bet he sees a lot of dates here.

She couldn't help but wonder if asking him for his opinion might be a good idea. Weren't bartenders supposed to offer good advice?

Then he returned to her end of the bar.

"Can I get your professional bartending opinion?" she asked while the Valley of the flowers was working its magic, leaving her feeling decidedly bold.

He collected her empty glass and began to unload clean shot glasses on a shelf under the edge of the bar. "I'll do my best," he replied.

God that accent was going to kill her. She shot a glance at the large hands that had delicately created an elaborate drink a few minutes earlier. There was no ring on his ring finger. But he had a Celtic band around one thumb. For some reason that sent her body burning so hot; she couldn't help but picture him gripping her hips hard, leaving the imprint of that ring on her skin as they made love.

"So... How do you know if the guy is...you know... right for a woman? I keep thinking men sound great when we chat on the app, but in person things just fizzle out. Is it my fault? It feels like it is." She hadn't really meant to ask him that last part, but it was the truth. Her date tonight had been attractive, and she should have wanted to kiss him, but it had died somewhere between the first awkward greeting hug and the ordering of the drinks.

The bartender straightened and looked her over before he spoke. His voice was smooth, deep, and so damn sexy it made her clench her thighs together. "Chemistry between a man and a woman cannot be conjured up like a magic trick. You either have it or you don't."

"So how do you know for sure if the chemistry is there?" Aubree pressed. After the dozen or so dates with different guys so far, she hadn't felt chemistry at all, at least not in person. While she didn't want to marry a guy just because they had good chemistry, she wasn't about to marry a man who didn't sexually excite her at all.

"How?" He leaned over the bar and gently tucked a lock of her auburn hair behind her ear. His fingertips lingered against her skin. She shivered with longing as something stirred to life within her.

"It can happen with a single touch, even a look." His voice was rich like the whisky he had poured in a short crystal-cut glass. His eyes swept down her body in a slow way as though he was removing each piece of clothing from in his mind. She could almost feel his hands touching her, peeling off her black cocktail dress, sliding off her black pumps, and caressing the cups of her bra before he—

Aubree jerked her gaze back to his face.

"You felt something just now, didn't you?" he asked, an all-too-knowing smile resting on his lips.

"Maybe," she admitted, glancing away in embarrassment. She had shared her hopes and dreams with *Long-Island23* for two weeks, yet she felt more with this bartender than she had with any other man in a long time...maybe ever.

"If you didn't feel the spark with him, it's not your fault. He's just not the man for you." He paused, as though he wanted to say more, but a man at the end of the bar waved him down. He answered the man with a quick nod and then turned to her. "Just a minute." Then he walked away to take the man's order.

The moment he was gone, rational thought returned. Aubree took advantage of the bartender's distraction. She grabbed her purse and quickly ducked outside. She pulled her coat on, walked across the street, and headed toward her apartment. Her heels sunk slightly in the inch of snow on the sidewalk; she wasn't cold at all though. In fact, she felt hot enough after that bartender's look, that she was surprised steam wasn't coming off her. She didn't even know his name, yet the scorching look he'd given her had overwhelmed her in a way she'd never imagined. It scared her a little.

Once home, she kicked off her heels, changed into her lounge pants and an oversized sweatshirt, and made some hot herbal tea. For a moment she sat on her comfy leather sofa, her body still humming from her talk with the bartender. It was as though the part of her that had been asleep had stirred to life. She felt, as foolish as it sounded, like a princess in a distant tower awakening from an enchanted slumber, even without the man's kiss.

Maybe romance was possible for her. If she felt something with that bartender, she could still have a chance at finding love and passion again. She pulled up the Meet Cute app, perusing it for new guys. The problem with the app was that she couldn't see anyone's face. It was all anonymous until the in-person meet up. She had dated a few guys that hadn't been too inspiring in the looks department. Nothing like the bartender tonight. Aubree felt bad for such a shallow thought, but she didn't really want to date a man who didn't take care of himself.

She started swiping but her mind kept drifting to the bartender's face and the way he looked at her like he could have eaten her up and come back for seconds. She groaned and threw her phone on the floor.

So much for tonight. So much for love. Maybe she should just give up.

Matthew Lawson turned away from the customer he had made a martini for and glanced down to the far end of the bar. She was gone.

Aubree Cole...

He felt like a stalker for memorizing the name from her credit card, but he'd been fascinated with her. He'd seen her come in two hours ago and sit nervously in the cozy little two-person booth close to the bar. He watched as she'd tried to focus on her phone, then look at the drink menu long enough that she had time to memorize it. She had that intense and thoughtful look about her that he didn't see too much these days.

Matthew had also seen that cocky bastard in the five-hundred-dollar suit walk up and give her the most awkward hug ever witnessed. It was clear the man was put off by Aubree. She was sweet, sexy, and obviously successful. She had that polished elegant look of a woman who needed to look presentable every day for a complicated high-powered job, but she didn't overdo anything. Yes, whoever Aubree was, she was a very talented and intelligent woman—just his type.

Matthew knew he shouldn't get involved. He had moved from Australia six months ago to open the Love Potion #9 bar with his friend Will. They'd both felt

Chicago was the perfect city to open their bar. As a city, it had the right mix of business and pleasure. He wanted customers from both worlds to enjoy the unique cocktails they made here.

He knew he should be focused on business, not chasing women. But damn, he couldn't ignore Aubree. She was just that, *irresistible*. There was a delightful innocence to her. She wasn't jaded by life or love, not yet, not like him. She made him want to give love a second chance.

Hopefully she would come back.

THE OLD FASHIONED

One week later...

She was back.

Matthew straightened, squaring his shoulders as he watched Aubree and a man walk into the bar and take a seat at a two-person booth. She moved with purpose and excitement, her face beaming in a way that made a man envision that same smile when she was beneath him on a bed. Bloody hell, she looked good, so fucking good. He hadn't realized how much he'd been hoping to see her again until she'd stepped through the door.

His gaze traveled to the man she was with. He was different than her last date. He wore a tweed three-piece suit with brown elbow patches and a pair of glasses that were stylish, yet retro. He looked like a bloody professor.

Huh...

Matthew saw a waiter headed their way and caught the waiter's attention with a shake of his head. The waiter backed off. Matthew picked up an order pad and walked over to the booth. He stopped inches from them with his pad and pen ready. Aubree had her head buried in the menu and didn't notice him. Her date noticed though.

"We'll take two gin and tonics," the man announced and pried the menu from Aubree's hands.

"Is that what the lady wants?" Matthew asked quietly.

Aubree's face jerked up at the sound of his voice and her eyes widened. A slight blush bloomed in her cheeks. The way her gaze swept over him, pausing a little too long on his mouth, had him stifling a groan. The woman was sexy even when she wasn't trying to be. It made Matthew wish she'd come back alone.

"Is that what *you* want?" Matthew repeated to Aubree quietly.

"I......"

"Of course. I always know what my dates want." The man dismissed Matthew, but Matthew didn't move.

"Sure, gin and tonic. I'll give it a try," she murmured.

Matthew held in a sigh as he turned and walked

away. He met up with his waiter, Rodrigo, when he returned to the bar.

"What's up boss?" The young man nodded discreetly toward the table.

"I've got that table tonight, but I'll bring any tips I get and put them in your jar, okay?" He slapped Rodrigo's shoulder.

"No problem." Roderigo grinned and headed off to another table recently claimed by a group of lively University of Chicago grad students.

Matthew stalked down the length of the bar and kept a watchful eye on Aubree's table once he'd delivered their two gin and tonics. She and her date seemed to be in an animated discussion now. Maybe he had misjudged the man. Maybe he and Audrey were hitting it off.

An hour passed before the man stormed out of the bar. Aubree half rose from her seat as if she was about to go after him, but changed her mind and sunk back down in her chair with her shoulders slumped. Her lips quivered as she brushed a hand through her hair in a nervous gesture. After a few minutes, she collected her purse and stood. When she glanced his way, Matthew crooked a finger at her and pointed at the bar stool directly in front of him.

She hesitated so he repeated the motion more firmly. She finally came over and sat down.

"God that went over well," she muttered sarcastically.

Matthew chuckled. "Okay, what happened this time?" He reached for an empty glass as she talked.

"Well for starters, I do not like gin and tonic. Totally confirmed that tonight. *Ugh*." She made a face and Matthew laughed. He liked her animation. A lot of women didn't like to make goofy faces or even act silly. Aubree didn't seem to have that problem and he really enjoyed that. A playful girl was a happy girl.

"Okay, then what?"

"Well, he's into academics, which I thought was very interesting. He's a professor of linguistics. But when I told him what I do for a living..."

"Which is?" He prompted, hoping she would share more about herself.

"I'm the Director of Equities at the Chicago Board of Trade."

Matthew nodded and she continued. "Well, he started talking about how it was cute that I had such powerful job." She put air quotes around the word "cute" and her striking hazel eyes lit with an indignant fire. "And that when he marries, he wants his wife to feel good about staying at home. I mean I'm all for women staying at home if that's what the *woman* wants. Not because some guy thinks it's still 1950 and a woman should be waiting for her husband with a cocktail in hand and meatloaf on the table."

"You don't think a person should do nice things for someone they love?" Matthew asked curiously.

"No, that's not it. Being nice and doing something out of love is different. *Antiqueluvr78* thought that this was something to be expected on a daily basis. A gift like that should be a two-way street. I make you meatloaf one night, you give me the best foot rub ever or fresh cut flowers another night."

Matthew started preparing a drink for her and then laid a twisted orange peel across the top of the glass. With a grin, he pushed the glass toward her.

"What's this?" She accepted it, eyeing the brown liquid openly curious.

"An Old-Fashioned in honor of *whatshisname*?"

"*Antiqueluvr78*," Aubree said with a giggle.

"This is bourbon, a sugar cube, bitters and a thick cube of ice."

"Wow." She took a sip. "Not bad at all." Her smile was infectious, and he couldn't resist his own grin.

"So *Antiqueluvr78*. Is that a screen name or something?" He leaned on the bar as she held up her phone so he could see the screen.

The bubbly words Meet Cute appeared on the screen and her profile popped up a second later.

"*Sailorgurl18*?" He looked at her profile name. There weren't any pictures, just info about her life.

"I like to go sailing on Lake Michigan. I grew up in Maine around boats. My dad was a fisherman. He died two years ago and when I'm out sailing on the lake, it reminds me of him and I feel closer to him?" She blushed wildly. "I'm sorry, I shouldn't be pouring my heart out to a stranger."

Fuck it, the woman was killing him. Matthew extended his hand. "Hello, I'm Matthew Lawson, born in Perth, attended school at Cambridge in England, then the London school of Economics. Now... I bartend and part of that is listening to customers."

Aubree smiled, still embarrassed as she shook his hand. "Aubree Cole. I went to Princeton. Born in Maine and I love to sail."

"There, now we aren't strangers." Matthew nodded at her nearly finished drink. "Want another?"

She thought about that for a minute. "Yeah, why not. Surprise me." She settled deeper into the bar stool and watched him get to work.

Matthew muddled a strawberry in a shaker, added some strawberry and vanilla-infused vodka, a little St. Germaine, lemon juice, and some fancy habanero bitters before shaking and straining everything into a martini glass. He then topped the mixture with a splash of sprite and edible rose petals before sliding the glass toward her across the bar.

"Meet the Ms. Monroe cocktail."

Aubree giggled as she picked up the bright reddish-pink drink and sipped. "Flirty with a dash of heat." She licked her lips and Matthew's body went hard all over. What the hell was wrong with all these men on the Meet Cute app? Aubree was a man's wet dream. She was curvy, fucking gorgeous, smart, and most importantly, she was real and approachable. It was rare in attractive women. Most beautiful women he knew were guarded. They were used to people preying on them for their looks, so they tended to lock down their hearts and act more reserved. Aubree was much more open.

"I really like this." She drank another sip. "How did you end up a bartender?"

Matthew could hear her curiosity. "I love making drinks. I love helping people who might need a friend."

He didn't tell her that he was a part owner of this bar. He wanted her to see him for who he was: a man who like to serve drinks. If being a bartender wasn't enough, then he knew what kind of person she was.

"So, you followed your passion. I like that," Aubree said after another drink of her cocktail.

"Exactly." From the corner of his eye, he saw a man waiting for him at the end of the bar. "Hang on." He left her, hoping this time she'd be there when he returned, and saw to the other customer. He didn't dare look back at her, but the heat across his skin made him think she was watching him as he poured and served. When he finally turned toward her, she was finishing the drink he'd made her.

"Thanks, Matthew. You made tonight much better." She smiled at him and for a second, he forgot how to breathe.

"You're leaving?" Matthew knew he sounded like a hopeful kid and not a grown man in his mid-thirties.

"Yeah, I'm calling it a night. I only live a block away, but I don't want to be too inebriated to walk home."

"Let me call you a taxi," he offered instantly. It was a common thing to call for a cab when a customer had a little too much to drink.

"Thanks, but I'll be all right." She pulled on a knee-length elegant red cashmere coat. "I like walking in the snow. It's kind of nice with all the quiet and the way it muffles sounds—even the traffic." Her face reddened again. It was clear she wasn't used to talking about how things made her feel, at least not to strangers.

"Me too." he said quietly as their eyes met. "About the snow. It's nice. Like walking in an empty church. There's a solemn reverence."

"Yes, exactly." Aubree looked down at her feet and back up to him. "Well... I should get going. I'm sure I'll see you later."

"I hope so. Bring any more bad dates here and

drinks are on the house." He flashed her a smile and she grinned back.

"It's a deal."

When she walked away, Matthew felt as though she'd ripped off a small piece of him and was carrying it away in her hands.

Fuck, he was falling for this woman he barely knew. He glanced at his phone and suddenly had an idea. He opened the phone and searched the app store until he saw the Meet Cute app. He downloaded it and hit the "Create Account" button, then he searched until he found her profile.

He couldn't stop smiling. This was going to be fun.

THE FRENCH KISS

Three days later...

It was a bit after eight PM when Aubree's phone beeped. The little heart shape on her screen meant she had a Meet Cute notification. She opened the app.

"*Vesper1* has sent you a hanky-panky challenge," She read aloud.

Aubree snuggled deeper into her couch and pulled her cup of hot peppermint tea toward her. She tapped on the question mark icon next to the words hanky-panky to read more about what it was.

"A hanky-panky challenge is a steamy challenge issued by one user to another. The challenge can be completed in person or online with whoever the user receiving the challenge chooses. The user can ignore challenges or accept them."

"Huh..." Aubree hit the button to read the challenge.

"*Vesper1* challenges you to French kiss a stranger with an accent."

It was kind of cute; she had to admit she liked the idea. Maybe because the first guy she thought of was Matthew, the hot Aussie bartender. Aubree stared at the screen for a long moment with her heart racing wildly as she considered if she should accept or not.

"Oh, what the hell." She hit the green accept challenge button. Little kisses flew up on the screen. Aubree checked her watch and glanced outside her tall apartment windows. It was dark and snowy, but the walk to Love Potion #9 wasn't that far. She threw off her cozy blanket and headed to her walk-in closet. After trying a dozen outfits, she finally picked a dark green knee-length long-sleeved dress, black tights, and cute little black ankle boots. Before leaving, she pulled on her coat, a scarf and a knit cap.

By the time she reached the bar, it was almost nine PM and the place was full of customers. Aubree saw three bartenders, including Matthew, working hard to fill orders. She hesitated, half hidden behind a tall wall that separated the bar from the restaurant portion of the large room. Matthew grinned as he shook a metal shaker and poured the contents into two glasses before topping them with cherries and umbrellas. It was clear he truly loved his job. But it still puzzled her a little that a smart man like him had left the business world just to make drinks. But if someone loved something, shouldn't they do it? As tough as her job was, she liked it a lot. Its challenges were fascinating; the way the trading floors worked had always been so interesting to her.

Aubree wondered if she should go home since the bar was full, but as Matthew's eyes swept the crowd, he spotted her and lifted his head in a silent greeting. When she didn't move, he waved her over. Her heart gave another wild excited bump as she approached.

"Have a seat." Matthew nodded at the only empty bar stool and looked at her expectantly. His blue eyes were so bright and intense.

"Just water, for now." She blushed and ducked her head. How did a girl ask a guy to French kiss her? She didn't really want to do that in a crowded bar.

"You eaten dinner yet?" He called out over the hubbub of the surrounding customer conversations.

She shook her head. She'd actually forgotten about dinner tonight; she been busy working late at home on project for work.

"If you can wait ten minutes, I have an hour break. There's a great pizza place next door."

"Sal's?" She nodded eagerly. She loved Sal's deep-dish pizzas.

"Great." Matthew moved further down the bar to prepare more drinks.

Ten minutes later, he handed off his black bar apron to another young man and grabbed his charcoal gray peacoat from the coat rack behind the bar. He put a hand on Aubree's lower back as he guided her out the front door, and her body burned from that single touch. They walked to the restaurant next door and ducked inside as wind blew down the street, showering them with fresh snow.

Aubree laughed as she brushed snowflakes off her nose and her heart stilled when she looked at Matthew's face. His eyes were bright and clear, and his lips were curved in a playful grin as he pulled her up against him. She gasped, a little shocked that he would touch her like that, but she had to admit she liked it.

And then she saw the rush of people passing by them as they left Sal's. Was he was just trying to make room for the others? She'd hoped he wanted an excuse to touch her. Once the flood of exiting customers was gone, he continued to hold her against him, just a moment longer than was necessary. Her body responded with a rush of heat and excitement.

"Come on, let's grab a booth." He curled an arm around her waist as they moved deeper into the restaurant. The pizza joint was noisy at the far end where a few men were watching a basketball game. Matthew chose a booth in a quiet corner.

A portly waiter came over and handed them laminated menus.

"Could we split a pizza?" she asked Matthew.

"Absolutely. I'll eat just about anything," he said with a boyish grin.

She looked up at the expected waiter. "A medium pineapple and sausage pizza please."

The waiter didn't even bat an eyelash as he wrote it down and left.

"Okay. I've heard of pineapple and Canadian bacon, but sausage?" Matthew reached for his glass of water and took a drink.

Feeling impish, Aubree responded. "Well, what can I say? I'm a girl who loves to get her mouth around a good hunk of meat."

Matthew spewed out his water and Aubree couldn't resist laughing at him.

"Sorry, I don't normally crack jokes like that, but the look on your face was priceless."

The sexy Aussie actually blushed red almost to the roots of his hair. "You *definitely* got me." He winked at her. "Is this how all your other dates go?"

Aubree bit her lip before replying. "Is this a date?"

Their gazes met and she saw his expression was

completely serious now; there was a burning intensity in his eyes as he replied. "It can be whatever you want. Dinner with a friend, a date, or even just dinner with your neighborhood bartender."

Aubree relaxed. He was letting her choose how this relationship would go as though he sensed she needed some control over it. God, Matthew made her so at ease. Yet, he turned her on like crazy. Sitting so close in the booth, she couldn't deny the chemistry between them was more than just sizzling. Whenever he looked at her, she couldn't help but picture him kissing her, then pinning her against the wall as he made her feel small and feminine while he mastered her with his body. He looked like the sort of man who knew just how to send a woman over the edge again and again.

She straightened her shoulders and prepared to ask him her question.

"Well, friendly neighborhood bartender, I need your advice and maybe your help." There. That sounded logical, not too propositional.

He waited, seemingly patient to let her continue at her own pace.

"You remember the Meet Cute app I showed you?"

"Yeah."

"Well, they have these challenges you can issue to other members, like sweet or sexy challenges."

"Okay." Matthew leaned forward in his chair and rested his elbows on the table.

"I've never gotten one before and normally wouldn't accept one, but then I thought what the heck. It lets me choose who to do the challenge with." So far this was going okay. He hadn't run out of the restaurant screaming yet.

"So, what was your challenge?"

"To French kiss someone with an accent?" She ended her sentence as a question because she still expected him to get up and leave.

"Well, good thing you're taking me out to dinner after making a sexy demand like that." He teased her.

"Oh God, I'm sorry. I shouldn't have asked you that. It's just…" She floundered for words.

"Hey, I was only kidding." He reached across the table and grabbed one of her hands, holding it gently. "So, the challenge is just to French kiss?"

"Yeah, no biggie, right?" She tried to act like it was nothing.

"It can be. Kissing is important." His voice was low and soft, almost a caress. "A kiss can be light or deep, heartfelt, seductive, sincere or comforting. How someone kisses tells you who a person is." He met her eyes as he spoke and in that moment, she glimpsed a part of his soul—the part that believed in the magic of what love could be and that a kiss held the power to change the world, not just one person. The intense way he was looking at her was something she'd already dreamed of.

His words were poetic and potent in a way that somehow the idea of kissing him didn't seem so casual anymore. It was suddenly so much more than that. Before either of them could speak, the waiter brought their pizza and it was a lot easier to eat and talk about everything but a French kiss.

She learned a lot about Matthew. He liked rock music from the seventies and learned to ride horses on a farm in rural Australia where he grew up with his grandparents. His parents had died in a car accident when he was only eight.

"Do you miss Australia?" she asked.

He shrugged. "Sometimes. The place you live in for a large part of your life will always hold significance, good or ill. I still visit once a year. But I don't miss it as much as I thought I would. I've been so excited about starting my life here." He paused. "Bartending has become an important part of who I am. I love guessing what a customer's favorite drink might be. I love making pieces of art inside a glass and seeing someone's face when they take that first sip. It's an ephemeral thing, but not all wonders are endless you know. Some beautiful things are fleeting but no less stunning."

"I agree," she said. "Like butterflies. They are

incredibly beautiful, yet they last barely a season and then they're gone. It doesn't make their value or their beauty any less."

"Exactly." Matthew brushed his hair out of his eyes and an almost bashful look on his face stole her breath.

Aubree couldn't help but fall for him a little more each time he shared something about himself, and she loved watching the way his eyes lit up when he spoke with passion.

"What about you? What brought you from Maine to Chicago?"

"I really wanted to work in investments, stocks and trading, but I didn't want to live in New York. It's just not the right place for me. I visited Chicago during college and fell in love with the city."

"What do you like about your job?" Matthew reached for another slice of pizza. Aubree couldn't believe how well this was going.

"I love the excitement and knowing that when I'm involved on the trading floor, I'm dealing with assets from companies all over the world. It's weird, but it makes me feel connected somehow with the rest of the world."

"That sounds like a hell of a good job," Matthew agreed.

"It is. I work a lot of hours, but I enjoy it." She paused, feeling so comfortable with him that she spilled her deepest thoughts. "I just never realized how lonely I've been."

Matthew reached for her hand again. "I understand that. When I left Australia to go to the London School of Economics, my girlfriend at the time had to stay in Perth for her own career. We tried the long-distance thing, but it didn't work out. When I came back, she had married someone else and moved on. Sometimes passion has a price, but it can be worth it to go after your dreams."

"You're the first person to ever say that. I can't tell you how many times people have asked me if I would have done things differently in my life. It's like asking me if I regret dreaming." Aubree had faced so much frustration with people assuming she was unhappy as a single, career-driven woman. Feeling lonely didn't equate to unhappiness. Happiness was much larger and more complex than a single emotion.

"So now you're dating?" Matthew asked.

"Yep, trying to anyway." She laughed at herself. "I probably waited too long."

"Nonsense. Just relying on a computer program to match you isn't easy. Romance can't be fully discovered and experienced on an app. Sure, it can help you meet someone, but it can't create that spark." As he spoke, he brushed the pad of his thumb over her hand and she shivered at her acute awareness of him; their bodies were so close at that moment. His knees bumped hers under the table when he shifted and looked deep into her eyes. People always joked about situations like this, but when a man really looked at her the way Matthew was now, she felt incredible. She felt like the universe included only the two of them.

"You want to return to the bar and discuss that kiss?" he asked softly. His tone was so gentle, so seductive that she was tempted to beg for the kiss right there.

"Yeah," she replied, her heart racing as he paid for their dinner. When she tried to hand him some bills, he waved it away.

"A gentleman always pays," he intoned softly and flashed her a dazzling smile.

When they returned to Love Potion #9, things had quieted, and he resumed his post behind the bar. He began to make them a matching set of cocktails. She knew better than to ask. He would tell her soon enough the name of the creation he was mixing.

Matthew added gin, St. Germain, Aperol and lemon juice into a shaker with ice before he strained the drink into two cocktail glasses. He topped the concoction with sparkling rosé before he garnished it with an orange twist.

"Allow me to present... the French kiss." He passed her one and he took the other, then he led her to a private round booth that wasn't visible to anyone else in the restaurant. She slid in first and he followed, sitting beside her in the spacious curved seat.

"These are really called a French Kiss?" she asked

"Yes." His eyes lit up with mischief and she took a sip. Delicious tastes exploded on her tongue.

"Oh, wow. This is so good!" She took a bigger sip. He did the same, clearly enjoying this exchange.

"Are you allowed to drink and hang out with customers while you work?"

He chuckled. "I'm a good friend of the owner; he won't mind."

Aubree couldn't imagine a boss being okay with that, so she hoped he wasn't going to get in trouble.

"You still up for that other kiss?" Matthew's blue eyes were burning straight through her.

"Yes." She put her glass down. "Are you? I don't want to—"

Matthew leaned in and captured her lips with his, silencing whatever she'd been about to say. Every other thought left her mind as he kissed her. His mouth moved slowly, languidly over hers. He licked at the seam of her closed lips and she opened them for him. At that first caress of his tongue, she moaned. He flicked his tongue against hers, playful and sinful at the same time. He was exploring her, learning her tastes in all the ways she liked to be kissed. He made her feel as though she was the only person in the world. No man had ever made her feel like that.

When their mouths parted, he leaned in and pressed his forehead to hers while he curled his fingers around the back of her neck. Their breath mingled in the closeness of the private booth.

"Challenge fulfilled?" he asked, his voice rough.

"Most definitely." She wanted to ask him to repeat the performance just to be sure, but she never been that assertive in her love life.

"Matthew... I..." She stumbled over her own thoughts. "That was really nice."

"Just nice?" His eyes twinkled and it sent wild sparks of excitement shooting through her entire body.

"Amazing," she clarified. "You kiss like a god. There. You happy?" She returned with a teasing laugh.

"I'm only happy if you are."

God, could the man be any more perfect? He was killing her with sweetness.

"If you ever want me to fulfill any more of those challenges, I'll be right here." He pulled out a card from his pocket and slid it over to her. She saw his name and number along with the Love Potion #9 logo of a smoking martini glass that looked as though it held a bewitched potion inside.

"That's my cell." He brushed a feathery kiss over her

lips, collected their empty glasses, and returned to the bar before he pulled his black apron on. She grabbed her purse and waved goodbye to him before she headed home.

As she got ready for bed that night, she checked her messages one last time. A new hanky-panky challenge was there from *Vesper1*.

Labor of love challenge: *Take a significant other out to do something new and fun that requires a little bit of work. This is a chance to experience something interesting together. Real love requires a bit of labor.*

4

LABOR OF LOVE

"Who's the girl?"

"Hmmm?" Matthew glanced up from stacking pint glasses to see his best friend and business partner, Will Goodman, leaning against the bar with a smirk.

"The girl. Who is she?" Will repeated, his brown eyes glinted with mischief.

"There's no girl." Matthew insisted. The last thing he wanted was for his friend to make fun of him. Will had a new girl every week, but he knew that Matthew was a one girl kind of man.

"You were humming Metallica. You only do that when you're thinking of a girl."

"Shut up." He snapped, but Will kept grinning.

"Come on, man. Tell me who she is. I know you've been taking different shifts in order to see her."

"*One* shift. It was *one* time." He had issued the French kiss challenge a week ago and he still couldn't believe Aubree had accepted and come to him. He'd made one of his favorite romantic cocktails and shared one of the best kisses of his life. He could still feel her petal soft lips and taste the cocktail on her tongue... God, kissing her had been like a drug.

And I'm hopelessly addicted.

"Matt, seriously. I know you've been avoiding dating after what happened in Perth but come on. This girl might be good for you. At least tell me about her."

Matthew set the last of his glasses down on the counter. He knew he better tell Will something or his friend would never shut up.

"She came in here one night and I saw that she had a really bad date. The asshole left her with the bar tab. I struck up a conversation and she's incredible. Sexy, smart, and confident, except for her dating life."

"So, you're dating her now?"

"Sort of." He wasn't sure how to express what stage their new relationship was in.

"Sort of?" Will cocked his head.

"It's more like friends with some benefits at the moment."

"I feel like you're leaving some details out," Will said.

"A gentlemen doesn't—"

"Kiss and tell. Yeah, I know. You're a damn boy scout." Will mockingly groaned and rolled his eyes before he turned serious. "If you really like her, take some time off. The bar is doing great. We can afford for you to take a few nights off with the extra bar staff we have."

Matthew relaxed. The idea of a fun night off sounded great, but he hadn't heard from Aubree since he had sent the second hanky-panky challenge to her and he was worried.

"So, when are you going to see her again?"

"Not sure. I gave her my number and I'm waiting to see if she'll call."

The second he said that his cell phone pinged.

"I bet it's her!" Will chuckled.

"It's not." Still, he checked the phone and when he saw an unfamiliar number with the message: "This is Aubree Cole." He couldn't stop grinning.

"See? It's her. The universe is listening, my friend." Will slid onto the bar stool facing Matthew. "So, what did she say?"

"Don't know yet." Matthew watched the three dots appearing on the chat screen to indicate she was typing. A second later her message popped up.

"She's inviting me to a paint and drink night."

"A what?" Will asked, his look of bafflement comical.

"One of those places where you drink wine and paint a picture or something. Usually there are other people there." He had to admit he was a little disappointed.

Will used his hand to imitate a crashing plane including dramatic sound effects of an explosion. "Sorry bud but sounds like a strikeout. She's basically taking you to a chick thing. She's knocked you off the bed list and into the friend zone."

Matthew typed in a quick reply asking for details and ignored his friend. Aubree messaged back the address and a time for that night at eight PM.

"You okay with me leaving tonight at 7:30?" he asked.

"Sure, sure. Paint something nice," Will snickered. "Maybe we can hang it up in the bar."

"Shut up, asshole!" He laughed as he threw a towel at his friend. Will caught the towel and flung it back before heading toward the kitchen on the restaurant end of the bar.

Matthew worked until 7:30, then called a taxi to take him to the painting place. When the car stopped in front of the shop, he got out and cringed as he saw a dozen women seated around easels, wineglasses in one hand, and paintbrushes in the other. He had nothing against wine, women, or painting, but a man belonged nowhere near them when all three were combined.

"Matthew!" Aubree called out his name from the doorway. He rushed up the steps and inside the shop while she held the door for him. When she closed the door, he got a good look at her. She wore jeans and a soft white cashmere sweater that hugged her curves just right. Her hair was in lush auburn waves around her face and she wore just a hint of makeup. God, she was so fucking gorgeous.

"Hey..." she greeted softly as her lashes swept down across her cheekbones shyly.

"Hey..." He replied, unable to resist reaching up to bury his fingers in her hair. It glowed in the soft lights, rich and dark with hints of red and gold, like autumn leaves.

"Sorry, I didn't text you sooner this week. Work's been hectic."

"Never apologize," he replied. "I was worried I scared you off."

She bit her bottom lip and he fought off the urge to grab her hair and kiss her hard, maybe even bite that lip himself.

"You didn't scare me. You kiss like a dream." Her breathless response made him grin and lean down, feathering his lips over hers. Given enough time, he could show her all the different ways he knew how to kiss.

"Come on," she said, taking his hand. "We're in the back." She led him by the open room of women painting. They all paused to stare.

"Whew, girl. You're one lucky woman!" Someone called out. Heat rose underneath Matthew's shirt collar and he plucked at it as he passed the women.

"We aren't painting with them?" Matthew asked Aubree.

"Oh God, no. I'm not that mean." She laughed and pulled the handle of a roughhewn wooden door that opened into a private studio. But there were no easels, no paint, no one else. Instead, there were piles of wooden boards, stencils and paint.

"I thought this might be more fun." She nodded at the room. "We're going to make handmade signs. Does that sound fun?"

Actually, it did. Matthew loved working with his hands.

"Yeah, this is great." He let her lead him to a rack where he removed his coat and rolled up sleeves. Aubree pushed up her sweater sleeves and motioned for him to join her by the wood pile.

"Choose four boards and we'll sand them. Then we'll paint a base coat and choose a stencil set. After that, you paint your words in your second paint color over the base color."

"This is seriously cool." Matthew grinned. "So, what's the occasion?"

Aubree blushed. "I got another hanky-panky challenge."

"Oh yeah?" He remained calm and casual. He didn't want her to know yet that he was the one sending her the challenges.

"Uh huh." She continued. "This one is called labor of love. You are supposed to do a fun activity that requires a little bit of work with someone you care about."

"I like that." He selected four pieces of walnut wood planks and she chose maple, then they headed to the sanding station. They worked on sanding the wood planks, while talking and laughing as they prepared their projects.

"Oh! I totally forgot." She rushed over to a cooler by the door. "The drinks. Did you know there's a Labor of Love cocktail?"

"I do." He laughed.

"Of course, you do, Mr. Bartender. Want to show me how to make some?"

"I'd be happy to." He left his sanded wood in a stack and they both washed their hands in the. Then he helped her lay out the supplies for the drinks. She'd come well prepared.

"You muddle the basil, rosemary, lime juice and simple syrup in the mixing glass." He tossed in all the ingredients and used the bar spoon to crush them together as best he could. "Then you add the citrus vodka and two spoons of chartreuse before shaking with ice." He handed her the shaker and she completed the process. "Strain it into two highball glasses over more ice and stir in the club soda, then top with a bit of pomegranate juice and garnish with a sprig of fresh rosemary." He handed her one of the two glasses.

"I like this one," she said after a quick sip.

"Me too." He took a taste and nodded to himself. "So, we sanded. What's next?"

"We paint the boards with a base coat."

Matthew chose black as his under color and a white paint for his words. Aubree chose a light khaki for her base coat and black for her words. After they painted the base coat and waited for it to dry, they collected the stencils for the quotes they wanted to paint on their sights. They worked in a quiet but pleasurable silence as they laid their stencils down and painted letters upon the board. When they were both done, Aubree looked up at him from across the table in excitement.

"You show me yours first," he said.

Blushing she revealed her sign. It read: "Love is

friendship that has caught fire." The name Ann Landers was written beneath it. She had used different stencils for the words friendship and fire so they were bolder and cursive.

"Now you," she said, grinning.

Matthew turned his sign to face her, his heart hammering and his hands a little sweaty with nerves. She read the words aloud, her face glowing.

"I love her, and that's the beginning and end of everything. – F. Scott Fitzgerald."

When her eyes met his, he saw a heartrending longing in them and his heart flipped. He was entranced by her, this gorgeous, smart, and fun woman. Something intense, indescribable but overwhelming, flared between them.

"Matthew, would you like to get out of here?"

"What?" He was confused. He thought the night was going well.

"I mean, do you want to come home with me?"

Beneath the heat in her eyes, he saw vulnerability. She was afraid of rejection.

"Yes. More than anything," he promised.

Relief washed over her face. "Leave the signs. We can pick them up tomorrow when they're dry."

They packed the ice cooler and Matthew carried it outside and down to the curb while she hailed a cab. Once they were sitting next to each other, he reached across the black leather seat, clasped her hand in his and squeezed it. She squeezed his hand back and he felt like he was wrapped in visible warmth. Being with her was so easy. Had it ever been this easy with any woman before? If so, he couldn't remember.

When they reached her apartment, he helped carry the cooler into the elevator. She really did live just a block from the bar. Inside *his* building, in fact. When she got off on the same floor as his apartment, his mouth fell open in shock.

"What?" she asked as she inserted her key into the door.

"I live across the hall from you." He pointed to the door six feet away from her.

"You do?" She stared at him.

"Yeah... Talk about a small world."

"How come we've never met?" She opened the door and he stepped inside her apartment.

"Different work schedules, I guess. I stay up until three AM and don't leave for work until noon." He still couldn't believe the odds though.

"You can put the cooler by the fridge." She pointed toward the kitchen.

He set it down by the stainless-steel appliance and looked around her apartment. She had a cozy leather couch and a big flat screen TV along with a gas fireplace. There was a large desk covered with papers in one corner of a small second-half room just off the living room. Prints of famous paintings hung on the walls. No landscapes. Just people. It made him think that she really did love people and want to connect with them. She was so open, so warm. It fit. He noticed her watching him.

"I like the art." He nodded around at her framed prints.

"Thank you." Her gaze swept over him. "Let me take your coat."

He slid it off his shoulders and she hung it by the door on a decorative silver hook nailed into the wall. When she turned back to him, she was rubbing her hands together nervously. He didn't want her to be afraid of him. He crossed the short distance and took her hands in his.

"Hey, we don't need to do anything. I have no expectations."

Her lips curved in a small smile as she freed her hands from his and laid them on his chest.

"But *I* do." She whispered an instant before she stood up on her tiptoes to kiss him.

Passion radiated from within him, sudden and hungry, as he cupped her face. He held her as he kissed her back. Her hands moved up his chest to his shoulders and rested there casually, yet his flesh tingled at the contact. His senses spun as he breathed in her sweet floral scent. He moved one hand to the hollow of her spine and his fingers lifted the hem of her sweater so he could settle his palm against her bare skin. He tipped her chin back and trailed kisses down her throat, glad she wasn't wearing a turtleneck. A pulse beat steady in her throat and he nibbled her skin just beneath her ear. She groaned and clutched at him.

"Please, Matthew." She begged. "Bedroom. Now."

"You sure?" he asked.

"Yes." She pulled at the front of his shirt, ripping it open and sending buttons scattering on the tile floor. He pulled free of the ruined shirt.

"Sorry!" She gasped.

"Not to worry. I have a dozen more," he promised as she took his hand and led him down the short hall to her bedroom where she tugged him back into her arms for another kiss. This time she was more urgent in exploring and he savored it as he lifted her sweater off her body. After a moment, they were tumbling back onto her bed. Jeans, boots and socks were removed in a frenzy as they laughed between kisses.

Matthew leaned over her, tugging the cream silk bra cups down to expose her full breasts. She was gorgeous and he buried his face in the valley between the two peaks. Aubree moaned and arched her back as he took one nipple into his mouth and sucked hard. He slid his hands behind her, unclasped her bra, and dropped it to the floor. He licked the hardened bud before moving to the other breast. As he explored her soft ivory flesh with fingertips caressing down her legs and up her inner thighs, he got lost in the heaven of her sighs and shivery responses. Without another thought, he wound his arms around her waist and lifted her, carrying her over to bed. They lay side by side, breathing slightly heavier as they shared a deep, openmouthed kiss.

"You're bloody beautiful, Aubree." Not only on the outside, but within. He wished she could truly know how much he meant it.

When he kissed her and closed his eyes, he swore he could see her soul shining bright and calling out to him. It felt like *home*. It felt like the last time he'd driven between the gates of his grandfather's ranch with the horses running through the pasture and the wind whipping their manes while his grandmother was baking fresh bread in the kitchen.

Being with Aubree… It filled that mystery emptiness he'd felt since he left Australia.

"I want to touch you," Aubree reached for his boxer shorts and he rolled onto his back so she could pull them off. Her eyes widened as she caught sight of his erection. He chuckled and pulled her on top of him.

"Kiss me," he begged softly. She rewarded him with a hot lingering kiss that made him hard and even more desperate to have her. When she curled her fingers around his cock and stroked, it felt so good he thought he might die. Her name came out as a groan as he gripped her ass and his fingers fisted the fabric of her panties before he ripped them off her body. A minute later, he rolled her back beneath him and she parted her thighs, allowing him into the natural cradle of her body.

"You have a condom?" He whispered.

Aubree shook her head. "I'm on the pill. We don't need one if you're clean."

"I am," he promised.

"Me too." She ran her hands up and down his back and he shifted, positioning himself at her entrance. They shared a sound of pleasure as he sank into her welcoming hot depths. He threw his head back as he withdrew before pushing back inside her.

"Harder," she encouraged.

Matthew was happy to obey. He braced one hand beside her head and they gazed into each other's eyes as he claimed her and she gave him everything in return. It rocked him to his core to see her face burst with delight when her orgasm hit. Her inner muscles clamped down around him and he nearly lost his own control right then. Not wanting to rush and hoping he could coax another release out of her, he slowed his thrusts. Soft sweet words were whispered between kisses and he hoped she could feel how much he adored her.

She arched against him as her body contracted around his shaft and this time, he couldn't slow down. He listened to her sounds and when she cried out with a second climax, he roared as he let go inside of her.

Once their bodies stilled, he sank forward onto the bed and tried to catch his breath without crushing her. They were naked and tangled in the sheets; he couldn' think of anywhere else he wanted to be in that moment. Matthew adjusted his position so they lay on their sides; he was still inside her as he pulled her limp, sated body close to his. He ran a hand along her shoulder, down her waist, over her hip and upper thigh as he watched her panting softly and staring at him. Her skin felt like satin and he never wanted to stop touching her.

"No regrets?" he asked.

Aubree shook her head. "You?"

"No," he brushed the backs of his fingers over her cheek and her lashes fanned down.

"Tired?" he tried not to smile when she fought a yawn.

"A little."

"Sleep," he suggested gently.

"Will you still be here?"

"Do you want me to be?" God, he hoped she would say yes.

"Yeah, I do. That's not weird for you?"

"It's not, and I'll be here." He held her close until she fell asleep. He yawned and pulled the heavy throw blanket at the end of the bed over them both.

Tonight had been a labor of love in more ways than one and he'd enjoyed every minute of it. He was falling hard for this woman. Part of him was thrilled but another part of him was worried. Was he ready for a new relationship?

5

X'S AND O'S

Aubree opened her eyes a little after dawn, comforted at the sight of her own room, yet something was different. The world spun a little as she felt a muscled thigh pressed to hers and a heavy male arm wrapped around her waist. A man had draped his body over hers.

Matthew... She really had slept with him.

Holy crap.

She started to move but froze. What was she supposed to do? She wasn't sure what the protocol was after last night. She had asked him to stay the night, but had that been the right thing? Or was she letting herself get too entangled with her emotions? She should try to keep things casual between them, right? She was supposed to be getting out into the dating pool and seeing all the possibilities. Maybe it was a bad idea to be falling so hard for Matthew. She had only known him two weeks and yet she'd slept with him on what she considered their first official date.

Aubree pressed the back of one hand to her head and drew in a few calming breaths. Last night had been wonderful—so damn wonderful. From the making of signs and cocktails, to every sinful, wicked thing that followed. She didn't want it to be a mistake, but after so many years of not dating, she wasn't sure what to do.

"You okay?" Matthew's deep baritone voice was whiskey rough with sleep and the intimate sound made her body flush with heat.

"Yeah," she settled back down in bed and he moved closer before tucking her naked body against his more snuggly. God, this was more than nice. She could get used to this.

"Still all right that I stayed?" he asked.

She rolled onto her back and looked up at him. He had that sleepy look that made even a hard-edged, handsome man like him seem cuddly; the thought made her smile.

He traced the smile on her lips with his finger. "What's so funny?" He grinned back at her.

"Nothing."

"Tell me." He spoke so gently, so warmly that she

couldn't resist anything he would have asked of her right then.

"It's just..." She reached up to stroke his jaw, feeling the slightest stubble starting to grow there. "You're so intense, so masculine and sexy, and I love that. But I like this side of you too."

"*This* side?" he asked.

"Yeah, your cuddly side."

Matthew laughed. "Cuddly? Me?" He rolled onto his back, pulling her on top of him and she giggled as she made herself a human blanket.

"Now, this is nice," he murmured.

"It is." She agreed as she felt his cock harden between her thighs. She moved above him before gripping his shaft and slowly taking him inside her. Her body felt full in the best way.

Matthew gazed up at her with lust, but there was something gentle in his eyes—a sweet sort of desire that made her chest ache.

They made love slowly, gently. His hands rested on her hips when she leaned down to kiss him and their tongues gently dueled as he thrust inside her over and over. For a long blissful moment, she truly forgot everything outside of this gorgeous man and the bed they shared. There was only them and the magic of the heat and passion igniting between them.

Love is friendship that has caught fire.

Aubree melted into him as an orgasm rolled through her, slow and deep. The aftershocks echoed in a sonorous way that made her blood sing. He came seconds later, breathing her name with quiet reverence.

"Christ, you are amazing." Matthew murmured against her lips as she settled beside him.

"Thanks, so are you." She nuzzled his body and rested one of her palms on the warm skin where she could feel his muscled chest.

"What time do you have to be at work?" he asked. His hands ran up and down her back, stroking her in the most soothing, seductive way. Her body hummed with delicious warmth as his body relaxed every muscle in her. She hadn't felt this calm and sated in...well she couldn't remember how long.

"Umm... Today is Saturday, so not at all."

"Good. I was worried you might have to work on the weekends."

"Sometimes," she admitted. "But that's rare."

Matthew pressed a kiss to the shell of her ear. "How about we spend the day together? I want to know every-thing about you."

She laughed. "You can't learn *everything* about each other in one day."

"No, but we can try." He kissed her ear again and she let all rational thoughts that might have made her say no vanish.

"I surrender." She gasped when his hands tickled her waist.

She escaped and ducked into the bathroom where she frantically brushed her teeth and ran a quick makeup remover under her eyes and a brush through her hair. When she looked decent, she pulled on her shower robe and peeped through the open door. Matthew was lying on his back in her bed, hands folded under his head in the sheets pulling low on his waist. Ropes of muscle formed his abdomen and a V shaped indentation pointed down his pelvis to what lie beneath the blankets. How had she not licked and kissed those muscles last night or this morning? Men only looked that good in magazines or romance novels. Real men weren't this perfect. That meant Matthew had to have some flaws somewhere, right?

"You want company?" he asked with a sleepy chuckle as he slowly turned his face toward her.

Shit! He had to have seen her watching him.

"Er..." Her rational brain said no. But her rational brain was not in charge. "You can go again so soon?"

Matthew cast off the sheets and rose from the bed in all his naked glory. And he *was* glorious. Aubree just stared at him, all too aware of how unbelievably rude that was but there was no way she couldn't look.

"I can go again," he promised as he walked toward her.

She stumbled backward into the bathroom just as he got to her. She put her hands on his bare chest when he reached around her and hit the water handle to turn on the shower. Water splashed against the white subway tiles and she tilted her head back to look up at a very naked Aussie man in her bathroom. God, what a fantasy this was!

His hands toyed with the belt of her bathroom robe before he slowly unfastened the loose knot. She held her breath and her heart pounded in a wild excited rhythm as he parted the terrycloth fabric. Her breasts were heavy and hot when he peeled the robe from her shoulders and dropped it to the ground.

Matthew brushed his fingers over her nipples and she shivered. Steam warmed her back before she pulled him into the shower with her. She smiled shyly and ducked her head. He was so tall, well over six feet, and she liked the way he filled the space of the shower. The spray heated them as he ran his hands over her body.

They took their time exploring each other in ways they hadn't been able to before. She leaned forward and licked one of his flat nipples and he groaned, holding her head against his skin. He slid one hand between her legs to stroke her and she rocked into his fingers in encouragement.

"Favorite color?" he asked huskily.

"Er..." It was so hard to think when his hand was

playing with her so deliciously. "Green." She finally got out.

"What kind of green?" he asked, still stroking her. She pressed kisses along his chest until she reached his other nipple and bit it lightly.

"Evergreen," she finally answered. "Like Christmas trees. You?"

"Red," his lazy smile was pure male, and it made her belly quiver in delight. "Like cranberries." He reached for the bar of soap and lathered it in his hands.

"I love cranberry sauce." She leaned into his touch as he began to wash her.

"Homemade or canned?" He rubbed his lathered hands over her body, and she did the same, enjoying the simple act of washing each other.

"Don't laugh," she warned but he did anyway.

"Canned? The kind that just plops out onto a plate and you can even slice it?" His blue eyes were so bright and jovial that she couldn't be too embarrassed.

"Yes, that kind. It's great. I love it and I won't be swayed otherwise," she warned but she was smiling.

"Fair enough, I like it too. My ex used to give me hell about it."

At the mention of his ex she stiffened. She didn't want to think of him with other women. It somehow made what they were sharing feel less special because she knew he must have done this with others.

"Hey... What's wrong?" He tilted her face up and she looked into his eyes which were a soft, almost Wedgewood-blue now.

Flustered, she tried to pull away.

"Aubree, what did I say?"

"Sorry," she mumbled. "You haven't mentioned an ex before now."

"Oh..." Matthew pulled her toward him. "So, it's that time is it?" He was gazing at her so seriously, but there was a gentleness in him that lessened her anxiety.

"What time?"

"The X's and O's talk," he said simply

"What?"

"You know, like the song, X's and O's? It's also a cocktail by the way. Tonight, I'll have to make us each a stiff one."

She washed her hair quickly and he did the same.

"What do you want to know?" he asked.

He turned off the shower and got out first, handing her the first towel he could find, and she pointed at her cupboards with extra towels for him.

"How many women have you dated?" Aubree wrapped her hair in a smaller towel.

"I had one great love when I was younger, Lena. We dated from age thirteen until twenty-three. After her... there's been a few women, but they were only short flings." He was speaking so calmly of his love life and the first girl he'd loved that he wasn't with anymore. She was stunned. Aubree didn't know what to say. She'd never really had that. She'd dated a couple of men in high school and college but her feelings hadn't been returned to the same degree, so she'd never felt fully in love or like she'd been in a serious relationship.

"Why did you break up with Lena if you loved her?" She removed the towel from her hair and combed her fingers through the wet strands, trying to hide her trembling hands.

He leaned back against the bathroom counter, towel hanging loosely around his lean hips.

"I knew my life would take me away from Perth, from my home and family. I was okay with that. Lena wasn't. She wanted to practice law in Perth. We did our best to make a long-distance relationship work, but after a year we realized our hearts were in different places and while there would always be some form of affection between us, it was no longer strong enough to survive our diverging paths in life." When he looked her way, she saw the ghost of an old pain in his eyes and in the curve of his melancholy smile.

"Do you still love her?" It was a question she shouldn't ask; she knew the answer was only going to hurt her.

"First loves, strong ones, leave a mark, like a river running through a valley of stones over hundreds of thousands of years. It wears a path; it leaves grooves and redefines the rocks around it. While that love may be long gone, its mark is still there, defining any new love that might come through into one's heart. My love for Lena is like that. It left me changed. There will always be echoes of that love inside me. But no, I'm no longer in love with her." Matthew met her gaze, his blue eyes somber and serious. "I heard from my grandmother that she's married and a mother of two now."

"Oh wow." Aubree walked up to him and wrapped her arms around his neck. "I'm sorry."

"Don't be. I'm not." He grasped her waist and held her back. "She's happy and I'm happy for her." His gaze turned playful. "What about you? Share your X's and O's."

"I...don't have much to tell. I dated a few men and it's never been serious."

"Why not?" he asked.

She paused, thinking it over. "Serious is scary. Really scary. I don't know if I could surrender my life and happiness over to someone else like that. And the men I dated never seemed to love me the way I loved them. It's made me gun shy, I guess."

Matthew reached up to toy with a damp lock of her hair. That was one of a dozen things she loved about him: how he made her feel cared for with all those small touches, those little strokes or playfully intimate moments like this. He *wanted* to touch her and wanted to be with her.

"When you're really in love, it's not about surrendering; it's about sharing."

She wished she could explain to him that it never felt like that with those other men. She always felt they would take part of her away, a part she wouldn't know how to get back. That was terrifying. So she avoided love, avoided relationships, and focused on work. Meeting Matthew had made her want to change all of that though. And that scared her too.

"Are we talking about love?" she asked, her heart battering against her ribs.

"Maybe." He still held her in his arms as she trembled. "Whatever this is, let's not worry or rush. Let's take our time."

He sounded so calm, so casual, but she wasn't. She planned her life down to every detail when she could. The moment she felt herself starting to go down a rabbit trail of worries, he raised an eyebrow as he studied her expression and gave her arms a gentle squeeze before his eyes lit with fresh excitement.

"Let me take you out on the town. I want to show you the bar."

"But I've been to the bar." She chuckled and tilted her head, watching him.

"Not like this. I want you behind the bar making cocktails with me."

"Really?" She had to admit the idea being behind the bar with him sounded really sexy and fun. "Will your boss be okay with that?"

Mathew bit his bottom lip, hiding a smile.

"What?"

"My boss won't mind." He bent his head and kissed the tip of her nose. "But first, I'm making you an X's and O's drink."

"Day drinking is going to be a problem with you isn't it." She laughed. "What's in this one?"

"Some Patron XO, bitters, ginger bear, lemon juice, and a little cinnamon- orange blossom syrup."

Aubree laughed. "I swear you're making up these drinks."

He mockingly scoffed as though offended. "I would never! Google it, honey."

"Okay, Mr. Cocktail." She snickered.

"Mr. Cocktail?" He raised a brow and smirked. His arousal pressed against her abdomen through their towels.

"I'll show you a co"

She slapped a hand over his mouth to silence him and they both burst out laughing.

"I think we'd better get dressed or we'll never leave my apartment."

"I'll go change at my place. Meet you outside the hall in half an hour?"

"Sounds good." She stood on tiptoe and brushed her lips over his before she pushed him out of her bathroom and closed the door.

When she heard him chuckling on the other side, she leaned back against the closed door and sighed with a silly smile painted on her face. She liked Matthew way too much. What if he broke her heart?

Please don't let this be a mistake...

6

DROPPING THE GLOVES

An hour later Matthew walked with Aubree toward Millennium Park. They meandered through the beautiful snowy pathways on their way to the skating rink that was built into the center of the park during the winter. At the moment, a hundred people were out on the ice skating slowly in graceful circles.

"You ever skate here?" he asked.

"No." Aubree blushed as she looked from him to the rink. "I don't actually know how."

"Then I'll teach you." Matthew led her toward an indoor stand that rented skates.

"Oh, I don't know..." She hedged.

"What's the worst that could happen?" Matthew played with her hands, lacing his fingers through hers.

She brushed her hair back from her face. "Well... I could fall on my butt and everyone would laugh?"

Matthew pulled her close, sliding his hands into the back pockets of her jeans as he held her against him and leaned down to whisper in her ear. "Then I fall with you and we laugh at ourselves. No big deal."

He could see the fear in her eyes, the fear that she couldn't plan or control this, but she needed to learn that life sometimes went off course and a person couldn't plan for everything.

"Okay." She still looked uncertain, but he kissed her and led her over to the stand where he paid for two pairs of skates. His were large and black; hers were dainty and snow white. They sat down on one of the bench areas by the rink's edge and changed out of their shoes. After leaving their shoes secured in a little locker, they made the awkward march on the skate blades together toward the ice. He told her that he'd played ice hockey in his youth, so he could help her stay steady and teach her how to skate.

He stepped backward onto the ice and held out his hands like he wanted to coach a newborn foal into walking at his grandfather's ranch.

"Come on, Aubree. You can do this." He waited as she placed her gloved hands in his.

"Keep your body weight balanced over your leading foot. Think like a penguin, okay?"

"A penguin?" She stared down at the ice beneath her skates with adorable skepticism.

"Yes, those little fellas in the tuxedos." He teased her and she looked up at him, smiling but still nervous. "They shuffle and keep their weight balanced, their center of gravity over their sturdiest weight-bearing foot at a time. Humans slip on the ice because we are used to putting our weight on the foot stretching way out ahead or behind us. So be a penguin, love."

He held her hands as she shuffled away from the safety of the rink's walls. He continued to skate backward, using his body's momentum to pull her along with him. The moment she got more confident, he could see the tension release from her body as her face relaxed. Her pursed lips softened as she breathed deeply and small clouds puffed out in the cold air. Snowflakes began drifting down here and there, growing thicker and thicker until people around them started laughing and pausing to catch the thick flurries on the mittens.

Aubree focused on her skating and Matthew kept her hands in his as she grew bolder and bolder.

"That's it. See? You're a natural."

Her lips were moving slightly as though she were talking. When he realized she was saying "be a penguin" over and over under her breath, he burst out laughing.

"Shut up!" She laughed too and almost stumbled. He immediately caught her, steadying them both. She tensed in his arms, but he rubbed her back to calm her again.

"You fall, I fall." He reminded gently and she buried her face in his chest. He smiled and wrapped his arms more fully around her before he pressed his mouth against the soft auburn crown of her hair. She smelled of vanilla and honeysuckle from the shampoo and conditioner in her bathroom. His smell matched hers since they had shared the bathroom this morning, but it was different than when it mixed with her natural scent of fresh and clean mixed with the snowy breezes coming in off the lake.

They skated for another half an hour until he could see her legs were shaky from exhaustion. Skating required use of specific muscles and since she'd never skated before, he knew she would be sore tomorrow. It was nearly lunchtime when they changed out of their skates and left the park.

"You hungry?" he asked as he reached for her hand and they walked toward the street.

"I could eat," she said with a relaxed grin. "That was fun. I'm glad you talked me into it."

"Me too." The snow was still falling and the air felt colder. Matthew wanted to take her someplace cozy and warm.

"You ever eaten at Park and Field restaurant?"

"No, but I've heard it's good."

"You'll love it." He hailed a cab to take them to Logan Square.

Park and Field was a local family-owned restaurant that featured classic farm to table cuisine. It reminded him of his grandparents' farm with the fresh food, the locally brewed craft beers, and the comfortable spaces to dine and drink. There was a large fireplace and dozens of deep leather sofas to sit in comfortably for hours. Upon arrival, Matthew chose a roughhewn wooden table close to the fire and the waiter brought them menus.

"Everything is good here," Matthew said when he saw her carefully studying the menu. When the waiter returned, he ordered a French dip sandwich and Aubree ordered a pan roasted chicken sandwich.

The man waiting on them wrote down their order and asked, "Anything to drink besides water?"

"What's your recommendation Mr. Cocktail?" Aubree asked Matthew.

He grinned. "Dropping the Gloves."

"Um..." Aubree glanced back at the drink menu. "Dropping the Gloves, then."

"Same for me," Matthew said.

Once the waiter left Aubree looked back at the menu.

"So, Russian vodka, apple cider, cinnamon simple and ginger beer?"

"Yep. I hope you like it." He had a feeling she would.

"Me too." A crimson blush stained her lovely cheeks.

"So, no real boyfriends. Nothing serious?" He continued their earlier conversation.

"Not really."

"And the dating app, it's been unsuccessful?"

"So far, I just wish…" She hesitated.

He didn't press her and didn't push for answers. He wanted her to feel comfortable enough to talk in her own time.

"Why is it so easy with you?" she suddenly asked.

"Is it?" He hadn't wanted to assume, but it was easy —*amazingly* easy to be with her.

"It is…" She seemed to still be puzzling that over in silence when their drinks and food arrived.

"Maybe that's a good thing," he said with one small, but utterly sweet, smile.

"Maybe so," she replied.

As they ate, he peppered her with questions about her life. She was an only child but had a dozen cousins from her parents' siblings and most of them still lived in Maine.

"The holidays are loud but fun. Never a dull moment." She added with a bemused look. "How about you? Your grandparents raised you, right? But no cousins?"

"None," he said with a rueful smile. "When I went to England for University, I met an American and we became like brothers. But we're nothing alike. He lives here in Chicago. You have to meet him soon."

"What does he do?" Aubree asked between bites of her sandwich.

"He's in the bar and restaurant business. We have similar tastes and interests." Matthew finished his French dip sandwich and polished off his cocktail. Between the vodka cider drink, the warm fire, and Aubree, he really had no desire to go anywhere. He could have stayed here with her forever, drinking good cocktails and just talking.

"Want to play a board game or something?" He nodded at a stack of used boardgames sitting nearby.

"Sure, I haven't done that in ages." Aubree went over to the table and sorted through the games. She returned with one under her arm called Masterpiece which involved looking at famous works of art and trying to guess their value by bidding against one another at auctions.

"No checkers or chess?" He teased.

"I'm not great at either of those," she admitted. "I don't like games that involve a ton of planning and strategy. This one," she tapped the cover of masterpiece. "It is one of my childhood favorites."

Matthew ordered two nonalcoholic apple ciders while they set up the game. As they played, he realized quickly Aubree knew this game very well.

"I think…" He grinned. "You rigged this so you can win." He tugged her by her waist onto the leather couch by the fire.

"Maybe," she admitted with a devious chuckle that made his heart melt and his body tighten with sexual hunger. She relaxed into his hold as he settled her on his lap.

"Enjoying the day so far?"

"Yes, definitely." She gazed at his lips and he was completely riveted. She was perfect. Perfect in a way that Lena hadn't been. He didn't know what to make of that. Strangely, it made him nervous because he was far from perfect.

"What's the matter?" she asked quietly while she smoothed his brow with her fingertips as though trying to banish his worries.

"You're so perfect," he said quietly. "And I'm worried that when you realize I'm not…"

Her nose wrinkled adorably. "Not perfect? Okay, what's the worst thing about you?"

"I leave clothes everywhere. I can't cook at all. And I'm pretty sure I could burn the water."

"That would be called boiling." She cut in with a giggle. "I can't cook either. Maybe we could take a cooking lesson together if you want?"

"I'd like that," he replied and traced his thumb over her bottom lip and her cheek. There was a calmness to the moment. It felt strangely infinite, as though this peace and serenity between them could somehow last beyond their final breaths. This moment would still be here long after they were gone. He could only hope that what he felt for her right now would last too.

"Don't take this the wrong way but I'm glad your dates sucked because it gave me the chance to meet you." He wanted to get on his knees and thank all those idiots who'd not seen how amazing she was.

"Me too," she leaned in and kissed him, soft and sweet. He returned the kiss, holding her safe in his arms as he made a silent vow not to screw up whatever beautiful thing this was. Her lips parted and he drew her breath inside him, overwhelmed by the intimacy that came so easily between them.

After a moment, he broke the kiss, holding her still. "You want to keep me company at the bar for a few hours?"

"Yeah." She kissed him again before sliding off his lap. They put away their boardgame and paid for the food and drinks before heading back out into the cold streets. Tonight, Matthew wanted to show her his world and woo her in the way he knew best...with love-themed cocktails.

Aubree spent an hour helping Matthew prepare drinks behind the bar along with another bartender named Jenny. Aubree knew she would never tire of watching Matthew in his element with the way he engaged customers and the looks of delight and appreciation as he delivered finished drinks. When he had to mix a cocktail in a shaker, Aubree got a nice view of his muscled arms as he worked. He kept his sleeves rolled up on his shirt and she saw that tanned skin, so golden and enticing. Even in the middle of Chicago winter, he somehow found sunlight. She wondered if maybe his bed lay in front of the tall windows so that when slept during the morning hours, the sun warmed and tanned his skin. She wanted so badly to see if that fantasy was true, and if it was, she wanted to lie down beside him and sunbathe like a cat... after he'd made love to her all night.

"Girl, I've seen that look before." Jenny said as she came over to Aubree and grabbed a tub of fresh lemons to slice.

"Hmmm?" Aubree had to force her gaze away from

Matthew and on to Jenny. The other bartender was slender with short, black cropped hair, and she had a few interesting tattoos at the base of her neck that looked like crows in flight. She'd kept Aubree laughing while they worked by sharing stories of Matthew tending the bar.

"Matthew is catnip. He's irresistible." Jenny laughed. "And you've got it bad for him. I can't blame you. He's really good for business. So many women who wouldn't normally order cocktails come over to the bar just to see him."

Aubree's face flamed. "Does he date the other woman he meets here?"

Jenny patted her shoulder. "No. Not at all. A lot of women have tried to get his attention. One woman even left her panties here at the bar with her phone number scrawled across the ass part with a sharpie.

"Seriously?" Aubree couldn't imagine leaving her underwear like that in public...for a man.

Jenny laughed. "Seriously, you have nothing to worry about. You're the first girl he's let back here too. He really seems to like you."

Aubree relaxed and when she saw Matthew watching them, he flashed her one of those panty melting smiles before turning back to his customer. When he was done, he came toward her and Jenny.

"Jenny, hold down the bar for a few minutes. I need to unpack some of the beer delivered yesterday."

"No problem." Jenny moved to the center of the bar and Aubree kept near Jenny in case she needed help.

A tall, golden-haired man in an expensive three-piece gray suit strode right up to them. He had those bad boy looks like Matthew, but unlike Matthew who turned out to be a total teddy bear inside, she sensed this man was a dangerous heartbreaker.

"Hey Jenny," the man greeted with a rakish grin.

"Hey boss."

Boss? Aubree flinched. This had to be Matthew's employer. She had to get out from behind the bar before she got him in trouble.

"Who's this?" he asked, his brown eyes settling on Aubree with clear interest. He had the word "player" written all over him.

"This is Aubree, Matthew's girl."

"Oh, I'm not." She hastily left the space behind the bar. "I'm so sorry. I shouldn't be here. Please don't fire him."

"Fire him?" The man tilted his head as he looked at her. And he seemed to register what Jenny had just said. "You're *Matt's* girl? No kidding! He was telling me all about how he saved you from some real dating disasters. Lucky for you that he was around, eh?" The man chuckled, still smiling. "You're definitely not the first woman he's bailed out of a bad date. He's got a real knack for picking up women stranded on dates."

Aubree felt like an invisible fist just punched her in the chest. Matthew had told his boss about her? He'd said he rescued her like some pity date?

Oh God... Was she a game to Matthew?

"I really should go..." She grabbed her coat where it lay on the bar along with her purse.

"Aubree wait!" Jenny called after her.

"Tell Matthew..." She started to say something and shook her head and fled out of the bar. She didn't go home. She just hailed a cab and had him drive her to Park and Field. She needed to think... She needed to escape the tight knot of pain growing inside her before it consumed her.

HANKY PANKY

"Where's Aubree?" Matthew asked Jenny as he came out of the storeroom with a case of craft beers in his arms. Jenny was scowling, one hand on her hip.

"Ask *him*." She pointed at Will who stood by the bar looking like a chastened schoolboy.

"What did you do?" Matthew asked. When he saw Will's deepening chagrin, he repeated more firmly. "What did you do?"

Will raised his hands in surrender. "I guess I put my foot in my mouth."

"Where's Aubree?" Matthew repeated in a low growl as he slammed the beer case onto the counter.

"She left," Jenny said. "After he," she jerked her

hand at Will. "Made a wise ass comment about you rescuing Aubree from some disastrous dates. He made it sound like you were pity dating her."

"I was being funny." Will grumbled as he slumped into a bar stool. He took one of the beers from the case in front of him and popped the cap using the edge of the bar before taking a long drink.

"Dammit, Will." Matthew cursed. "I like her. A lot." He turned to Jenny. "When did she leave?"

"A few minutes ago. I think I saw her get into a cab."

Matthew snatched his coat and shot one more warning glare toward his best friend before he rushed out into the snowy night.

"Aubree!" He shouted her name, but the streets were mostly empty, and he didn't see her, which meant she must have gotten into a cab like Jenny thought.

Thinking she'd gone home, he ran the block back to their apartment building and went straight to her door. He knocked a dozen times, but either she wasn't there or she didn't want to answer. He pulled his cell phone out of his coat pocket and dialed her number. *Nothing.* No answer. He waited for her voicemail to beep.

"Aubree, please call me back," he said.

Matthew stood in the hallway for what felt like forever before he turned to face his apartment just across the hall. His shoulders slumped as he headed inside. How the hell had Will wrecked this so fast? And how the hell was he going to fix it, assuming he could?

He pulled up the Meet Cute app and signed into his account, then he examined the hanky-panky challenges, looking over his options. This might be the last way to reach her since she didn't know who had been sending her the romantic challenges. It was one last thing he could try. He chose the "Design your own hanky-panky challenge" and crafted it carefully and hit send. Now all he could do was wait and have faith.

Aubree was sitting by the fire in the Park and Field restaurant, a mug of warm apple cider in her hands as she stared off at the flickering vermilion flames. Despite the cozy warmth of the restaurant, she felt numb. Empty. Cold on the inside and out. A chasm had opened inside her chest and darkness was slowly spreading through her from that bleak fissure. She'd fallen in love with Matthew. Too fast. Too foolish.

Her phone pinged and she almost ignored it but finally curiosity got the better of her. She winced when she saw was a Meet Cute app notification. She clicked on it and saw *Vesper1* had sent her another challenge.

Whoever this *Vesper1* was, he had sent her a string of fun adventures that had ended in heartbreak. Her finger hovered over the delete button before she finally tapped read.

Hanky-panky challenge: Love is friendship that has caught fire. If you still believe this... Give love a second chance. Give me a second chance.

She stared at the words. *Give me a second chance?* But

...

"Oh my God..." She murmured. She didn't know *Vesper1*, he just sent her some messages for the challenges, that was it. But every challenge had led her to Matthew. She was torn between fury and confusion. Was Matthew the mysterious online user *Vesper1*? And if he was, why had Matthew used the app?

Aubree closed her eyes, remembering all the wonderful moments she'd had with him and how everything had been destroyed by one man's stupid comments. Was she really going to walk away from Matthew without an explanation at least? She owed him that, but she also owed herself. She hit the accept button on the challenge and replied to *Vesper1*.

"Meet me at millennium Park in 20 minutes."

She paid for her drink and hailed a cab. When she got to the park, it was filled with people and light. Snow flurries were falling from the skies in delicate swirling patterns making the night feel strangely intimate. She smiled as a couple of children in thick coats and brightly colored knit caps rushed past, shouting about building snowmen. Their beleaguered parents trudged behind them, carrying steamy cups of coffee. Ahead of her, the park was full of people enjoying snowy night and the skating ring in the distance was lit with sparkling white lights.

The closer she got to the rink, the more she could make out in the snow. A man stood with his back to her, his gloved hands braced on the walls of the rink. His dark blond hair was lightly dusted with snow, but she would recognize him anywhere.

"*Vesper1*?" She spoke the screen name and the man turned.

Matthew stood before her, pain in his hauntingly beautiful blue eyes.

"Aubree... Please let me explain and if you still never want to see me again, I understand."

She nodded, keeping herself a few feet away from him. If she came any closer, she would be tempted to run into his arms, but she needed answers.

"That night you showed me the Meet Cute app, I decided to create an account. I liked you. More than liked you. That first night we met, I wanted to find a way to make you come back, but I was also worried you might not take me seriously. Most women in high-powered jobs don't want to date a bartender. So, I used the app to find you and send you the challenge. I knew you could have gone anywhere to do them, but I hoped you would come to me. You did and as crazy as it sounds, I fell in love with you. After Lena, I never thought I'd fall in love so hard and fast again, but I did with you." His lips curved in a soft, slightly surprised smile that threatened to break down every wall she'd tried to build in the last few hours. He cleared his throat and continued.

"Will, that man in the bar, that idiot who speaks without thinking sometimes, I told him about you, about how I met you. Will always says the wrong things at the worst times. I never thought you needed rescuing and I didn't do any of this out of pity. I did it because I liked you and I wanted to be with you."

Aubree processed everything he said, a little stunned. Okay, *way* stunned. "Did you get fired?" she asked quietly.

"What? No... Will can't fire me."

"He can't? But Jenny said he was the boss."

Matthew smiled a little. "Of her, yes. But not me. You remember I told you that my best friend was here in Chicago? That was Will. He and I both co-own Love Potion #9 together."

"What? Why didn't you tell me?" For some reason that upset her too. It was another deception.

"I didn't tell you right away because I wanted you to

like me for *me*. Unlike Will, I like doing the work behind the bar. That will always be part of who I am, and most women think that kind of job is temporary. I love making drinks, love talking to customers. I like staying engaged in the human experience. I wanted you to see that part of me first before I showed you the business side of me."

Aubree was silent, still processing everything he'd said. So, he was the owner of the bar, but he was afraid she would judge him if he was just a bartender? She could understand that. After all, she had wondered why he tended bar when he he'd attended Cambridge and the London School of Economics.

Matthew held out a hand to her. "Will you give me a second chance? Please?"

Aubree gazed into his eyes, seeing only honesty and a tender hunger for her. A hunger that echoed the loneliness and desire within her own heart.

"If you want me, I'm yours, Aubree. You remember that quote I put on my sign? I meant every word and I was talking about you. I love you and that's the beginning and the end of everything."

Aubree bit her lip hard as her eyes burned. She was so afraid to believe in magic of love anymore. She was afraid to trust her heart, yet she'd began this journey to find love. What kind of person was she if she turned her back on it now? Her friendship with the sexy Australian bartender had indeed caught fire and she wanted those flames to burn even brighter. With a trembling hand, she touched his gloved palm and he pulled her slowly into his arms, the embrace full of fire and tenderness.

"I'm afraid of getting hurt," she whispered as he nuzzled her cheek. His soft, delighted sigh filled her heart with a blinding tightness and cottony warmth.

"Me too," he said. "But it's worth the risk. I feel deep inside that you are the answer to every question I'll ever ask. I never thought I could fall in love again this hard and fast, but I don't regret a second of it."

Aubree couldn't stop the tears that followed as she clung to Matthew. "How is it possible to feel like I've loved you and missed you my whole life, even though we've only just met?"

Matthew cupped her face in his hands. "Aristotle once said love is composed of a single soul inhabiting two bodies. I believe we've finally connected our two missing pieces."

A hot ache burned her throat as she pulled him down to kiss her. Explosive currents danced between them when their lips met. Snow stung her cheeks in wintry kisses. Aubree didn't want to be anywhere else in that moment. The magic she'd forgotten to believe in long ago pulsed, and soft, seductive intimacy formed between them as their mouths met over and over in slow kisses.

"You are the beginning, the end, my everything," Matthew murmured between fervent kisses.

"And you are mine." She meant it to the depths of her soul.

Love is friendship that has caught fire.

EPILOGUE

ix months later...

Warm white sand burned Aubree's feet as she stepped out of the shallows of the pure blue waters of the Bahamas and headed toward the white canopy bed tucked beneath a thick shelter of palm trees. Matthew stood by the bed, wearing a pair of pale blue board shorts that made him far too sexy for a public beach. Aubree was glad they'd splurged on a private bungalow overlooking the water at their honeymoon resort. She was still getting used to the elegant diamond ring and the wedding band on her finger, but she loved being married to Matthew.

"You cool off?" he asked as he wrapped her up in a red and white striped beach towel. He draped it around her like a cloak and pulled her to him for a kiss using the towel to keep her body pressed flush to him. She giggled against his mouth.

"Yes. But you're making me hot again."

"Good," he chuckled, that rich sound melting her into a puddle in his arms, then he ravaged her mouth. His hands released the towel and he palmed her bottom, squeezing lightly in a way that made her moan with delight.

"Matthew," she said when he finally let her breathe.

"Hmm?" He brushed his nose against hers. His arms banded around her as though he wished to never let her go.

"What is a Vesper?" she whispered as she kissed his neck and bit his earlobe. His skin was slightly salty from the sea and his dark gold hair was still wet, leaving the strands to curl a bit at the ends.

"A vesper?" he asked with his eyes still closed.

"Yes, what is it?"

"It's a cocktail."

"Of course, it is," she laughed again.

Matthew looked down at her, mischief and love in his expression. "James Bond invented the Vesper cocktail in the first Bond book *Casino Royale*. He named it after the first woman he ever loved: the beautiful and doomed Vesper Lynd."

"*Vesper*," she repeated. "One for his first love?"

"First and only," Matthew smiled.

"Could you make me one of those?"

"Certainly, but I have another drink in mind just now." He scooped her up in his arms and carried her back to the canopy bed.

The white curtains billowed out around them and the island breeze tickled her skin. He settled on the bed beside her and she couldn't resist touching him. She trailed a hand down his chest to his stomach, feeling his abdomen muscles clench beneath her exploring hands. He caught her hand and raised it to his lips for a kiss before reaching over to the bedside table where a brightly-colored orange and pink cocktail with a sassy looking little umbrella propped in it sat.

"Up for a new hanky-panky challenge, wife?"

"Always..." She laughed and sipped the drink. "What is it?"

"Sex on the beach." He was flashing her that naughty smirk that made her legs tremble in excitement and her womb quiver in anticipation.

"The challenge or the drink?" she asked.

"Both, my love. *Both*."

Thank you so much for reading Aubree and Matthew's story! If you want another swoony contemporary romance, be sure to check out Legally Charming where a workaholic attorney returns home from a business trip to find a woman in a princess costume asleep in his bed on halloween night - she turns out to be his little brother's friend and totally off limits to a man like him!

Turn the page to read the first three chapters! Or get the book now HERE!

LEGALLY CHARMING
CHAPTER 1

A man wearing only the bottom half of a *Star Wars* stormtrooper outfit streaked past Felicity Hart. She ducked out of the way as the half-naked frat boy whooped and bounced to the music, heading straight for a group of girls wearing white bunny ears who were gathered by the kitchen bar.

So this is what grad student parties are like.

Drinking, dancing, and insanity. Felicity shook her head, trying not to laugh. After growing up in a small town in Nebraska, she hadn't been prepared for college life in Chicago. Talk about culture shock. She was used to everyone in town knowing not just her name, but far too much about her personal life. Even after six years of living here, being surrounded by thousands of strangers who knew absolutely nothing about her, it was still both completely unsettling and oddly liberating.

For the first four years of college and the past two years of her master's, she'd hidden in her little shell. But a few months ago she'd met Layla Russo, a graduate student just like her, and they'd hit it off. Layla was the only reason Felicity had pulled a Cinderella and come to the ball. She would have laughed at the thought, but she was dead tired and stifled a yawn instead. At this rate, she'd turn into a pumpkin before midnight.

Happy Birthday to me, she thought and fisted her hands in the voluminous skirts of her Tudor gown. She stood out too much at this party—which happened when you skipped over the sexy cat costumes and zeroed in on the classy Anne Boleyn Tudor ball gown. Felicity should have worn some cheap costume, but she just couldn't do it. Halloween was her favorite holiday. She'd scrimped and saved to buy a good costume, one that meant something to her. She'd been lucky enough to find this gown on a deep-discount rack at a costume warehouse. Hence the beautiful, elegant, yet still sexy gown she wore at that moment. At least it had been sexy in the sixteenth century.

I am such a nerd.

She had gotten her share of raised eyebrows and

smothered laughs when she'd entered the apartment with her friends, but she didn't care. She was ready to celebrate her entrance into adulthood at a normal party. Even if it had taken her until graduate school to be brave enough to attend a social gathering like this.

And why shouldn't she? She'd worked hard—late-night study sessions, endless art exhibit submissions—all in the hope of attaining grades that would be good enough to take her from a small Nebraska town to the hip art communities of Chicago. She *deserved* a party. And going to one at Layla's boyfriend's fancy apartment was safe enough since it was close to the school and the gallery where she worked.

Several laughing girls bumped into her, plastic cups brimming with alcohol. She danced back a step, narrowly avoiding drenching her gown in cheap beer as one of the girls stumbled in her heels, sending her cup flying through the air.

"Shit!" the girl hissed, then started giggling with her friends as she bent over to clean up the mess.

The entire night had been one near miss after another. The last thing Felicity needed was her costume smelling like beer.

She glanced at the group of pretty girls in the bunny ears and the gathering of boys around them.

Why didn't I think of wearing something like that? She

glanced at the girls with their perfect bikini bodies, and she blushed. There was no way she could run around in something skimpy like that and feel confident. She just didn't look good in tight clothes...or revealing clothes. She was a size twelve, which was just a little too plump to look good in a skintight costume. She shuddered at the thought of being so exposed.

The crowd of people thinned out as she headed toward the room she sought. She took a moment to pause, one hand resting on the wall as she tried to suck in a breath. Maybe the corset was a bad idea.

"Hey!" A familiar feminine voice cut through the noise, and Felicity looked over her shoulder.

Layla was the official hostess of the party even though the apartment belonged to her boyfriend, Tanner, and she certainly acted like it as she strode toward her. She was a sight—five foot, curvy, and completely rocking her zombie stripper costume. Amazingly, Layla managed to look both scary and cute as she crossed the room in her four-inch stilettos. Felicity knew without a doubt that she'd break her neck in shoes like that, which was why she'd opted for red silk slippers that matched her gown.

"Hey, you okay?" Layla reached her and linked her arm through Felicity's. "I saw you yawning from across the room."

Felicity wrinkled her nose. "Just tired. Been up since dawn, have a midterm paper due tomorrow, and I feel every minute of a year older." Felicity wrinkled her nose. "Is it still all right to crash in Tanner's brother's bedroom?"

"Of course! I don't want you having to travel across half the city tonight to get back to that little hole in the wall you live in." Layla linked her arm through Felicity's. "I really wish you'd just move in with me." Her friend pouted dramatically, but Felicity stiffened her spine in an attempt resist Layla's begging.

"As much as I love your apartment, Layla, it's out my budget at the moment." It was double what her tiny place was, and Felicity's budget was already stretched thin. "You sure Tanner's brother won't mind?" It still felt weird to be sleeping in a guy's bed whether he was there or not.

"Yeah. Jared won't be back till Sunday night, so you're welcome to stay the whole weekend," Layla said. "Besides, even if he wasn't spending the entire weekend working, he'd never be caught dead anywhere near a party like this. That workaholic wouldn't know fun if it bit him in the ass." She snorted as though picturing just that. "Are you sure you're just tired, birthday girl?"

With her classes and her part-time job, Felicity was grateful for early nights where she could find them—

and the prospect of staying up into the wee hours and endangering her beloved dress didn't hold much appeal. No, the sweet song of a comfy bed and a few hours of oblivion was calling to her.

"I'm good!" she insisted. "Go have more fun and don't worry about me. Go find Tanner before he realizes you've ditched him." Felicity pointed to Layla's boyfriend, who was politely escaping the group of bunnies and searching about for Layla.

Tanner Redmond and Layla had hooked up the first day of classes five years ago and had been together ever since. He was hot, smart, and totally nice, not at all like some of the entitled jerks she had to deal with when she handled rich clients at the gallery where she worked, which was a shocker given that he was a rich kid. He and his older brother, Jared, shared this beautiful apartment. She'd never met Jared. Even though she'd spent the last three months around Tanner and Layla, the mysterious older brother had never once shown up.

Layla's dark eyes ran up and down Felicity with concern. "You sure you don't want to stay out here? You don't have to crash now. Unless you're not feeling well?" Layla cocked one hip, her hand perched there as she continued to study Felicity. Felicity swallowed down the flutter of nerves that always came whenever her friend tried to make her participate more in the student culture, but she shook her head. She wasn't good at being fun and spontaneous or wild. Graduate student life seemed to be built on those three things when one wasn't studying or writing papers. It was just her luck that she was too shy to be bold in life like Layla.

It never ceased to amaze Felicity how much of a mother hen her friend could be.

"I'm good," she answered Layla, her voice firm. Sometimes she had to use a "parent voice" in order to get Layla to stop mothering her. "Go and have fun. You said the bedroom is the last on the left?"

"Yup. And seriously, stay the weekend. Just come back here after your midterm, and we can hang out." Layla's offer was tempting, and Felicity found herself more than considering it. It sure would be nice to crash here for a few days. "I still can't believe you have a term paper due on the Saturday after Halloween," Layla muttered. "Ugh." Layla wrinkled her nose. "Some teachers are jerks. I'd be happy to make a voodoo doll of him, and we can shove pins in him." Her friend was grinning wickedly as she suggested this.

Felicity bit back a laugh. "If I didn't like Professor Willoughby as much as I do, I might take you up on that."

Layla escorted her all the way to the door and then

curved her arms around Felicity in a hug. Her throat tightened as she fought off the fierce happiness that came over her whenever her friend hugged her.

Layla didn't hug by halves—she gripped you hard, squeezed the air out of your lungs, and made you feel loved.

Felicity just wasn't used to that—unlike Layla with her sprawling and loud family that found it natural to hug and kiss constantly, Felicity's parents were not overtly affectionate. They were sweet, and she knew they loved her, but they didn't put their affection on display like Layla—unbridled and consuming.

"Just do me a favor. Get some rest and kick butt on your research tomorrow."

"Yes, *Mom*." Felicity stuck her tongue out, and they both giggled.

As Layla turned back to the party, Felicity slipped into the sanctuary and relative quiet of the dark bedroom. Her breath caught as she took in the view of the city through the tall windows. The skyline of downtown Chicago was a man-made mountain range of lights twinkling in a sea of black. The sky behind the buildings was a soft purple, cutting a contrast against the silhouettes of the buildings. It was one amazing view, and it always made her breathless when she caught a glimpse of the monolithic buildings. Her hands ached to sketch the sight, but she hadn't brought her pad with her.

Fifteen stories up, none of the city sounds that kept her up at night could be heard from Jared's bedroom. She liked that. She wandered over to the window, wanting to sate herself on the sight of glittering lights and an endless glowing horizon. When she'd had her fill of the view, she turned back to investigate just what sort of room she would be spending the night in.

A massive bed against one wall with a cherrywood headboard and a deep crimson comforter looked soft and inviting. The scent of aftershave and an enticing masculine aroma made her all too aware again that this was a man's domain. She scanned the rest of the room. A large desk was laden with files and paperwork. If he was such a workaholic, why didn't he spend more time at this desk and enjoy the view? If she had this to look at all day, she could see the appeal of working from home. But as a lawyer, maybe he didn't get that option, and had to be in the office all day.

It suddenly bothered her that she had no idea what Jared looked like. Being in his personal space like this was oddly intimate, and it felt strange seeing so much of the man without ever having seen his face. As an artist, all she did was think about what things and people looked like. Not being able to see the features or the build of the man who lived here was unsettling.

Layla had said he was thirty and panty-melting hot—but not as hot as Tanner, of course. Layla wasn't the type of girl to really eye another man when she was happily in love, but she did appreciate beauty of the masculine variety. Felicity had laughed at the thought. She'd never seen any guy worth calling panty-melting hot, at least none outside of the movies. Layla said that Jared could give Jamie Dornan a run for his money on hotness and intensity.

Layla's words came back to her, and she smiled as she could hear her friend's voice so clearly in her head. "You know what I'm talking about. Tanner is all sorts of brooding and intense. He can just look at you and you go all wet and melty, you know? Like he'd fuck you so good you'd break the bed and ask for more. Jared's like that, too." Felicity hadn't been able to get that out of her mind. Layla had said Tanner was just like Jared, only younger. It explained everything. Tanner's intensity was tempered by his youth and sweetness, but his older brother had that jaded, hot bad-boy thing going on, according to Layla.

Now she stood in said panty-melter's room and couldn't help but picture a gorgeous, sexy man walking through the room, putting on a suit, critically eyeing his appearance in the mirror over the dresser.

Unable to resist and knowing it was completely

inappropriate, she opened the top drawer of the beautiful dark dresser. Neatly rolled ties of a dozen different colors and patterns decorated the drawer, and a set of different styles of watches with leather and metal bands sat next to a box filled with cufflinks that glinted like jewels beneath the glass lid.

"Wow." She trailed her fingertips over the watches. A man with refined, expensive tastes.

Felicity watched the shadows play across the room, accenting the bed where Jared slept. What would it be like to share a bed with a man like him? To be the focus of all that raw masculinity and sexual energy? Her body hummed at the fantasy her mind seemed determined to play out. Her skin burned at the thought of what could happen if he came here tonight and found her in his bedroom. What if he just stood there, blocking the door, staring down at her? What if he told her to strip off her clothes and get into bed?

God, I need to get laid. Felicity shook her head. Even though she was a virgin, her fantasies could get wild. She struggled to get her libido under control.

Felicity sighed as she leaned against the bed, relishing the moment to bask in such luxury. She smoothed a hand over the red comforter. Satin? No, silk. She was tempted to lie down, just for a bit, but she knew she should change into her PJ's before getting in.

She tried the nearest door, only to discover a large walk-in-closet with dozens of suits and a tall rack of expensive leather shoes. Not the bathroom. Her bag was supposed to be in the bathroom where Layla had said she'd put it. She approached the last door she hadn't opened. Felicity flicked on the light, found her bag sitting on the marble floor, and then searched through her clothes. When she didn't immediately find them, she dumped her gym bag over, muttering as she dug through the contents on the bed.

"Damn!" No pajamas. She'd left them at home.

All she had was her change of clothes for tomorrow. She wouldn't sleep in those. Returning to the bed, she put a hand to her stomach. The corset dug deep into her. How the heck did women live like this back in the day? Sure, it was fun to wear for a couple of hours, but spend her life in one of these? No way.

Gathering her skirts, she tucked her legs up on the bed and rested her head on the pillow.

So soft. Her mind started to drift in that hazy place between being awake and being asleep. What would it be like to live in a place like this? Surrounded by beauty, success, wealth? She'd likely never know. Her dream was to be an artist and a curator of a museum. Not much money in either of those dreams, but they were her passions.

Passion.

The word made her smile. The man who slept in this room definitely had passion, workaholic or not. He appreciated the finer things, and his taste was impeccable. Her fingers tapped along the bedding. It really was a pity she'd never meet the owner. A yawn escaped her, and she stuck a balled fist against her mouth. Her thoughts drifted, and she let them wander into dreams of the sexy man whose bed she was currently in and what would happen if he returned.

Jared Redmond stumbled from the taxicab, his brown leather briefcase smacking his back as he struggled to stay on his feet. He swallowed a growl of frustration. This was the last time he let the senior partners of his firm keep him out late to celebrate. He'd only had one drink, since he was dead tired from the last few months of overtime at the office. Having to smile, laugh, and socialize all night with the partners left him edgy and desperate to get home and crawl into bed.

God forbid he just do his job and do it well enough to earn respect. No, he had to spend hours at one of the most expensive restaurants with them, watching them pat each other on the back when he'd done all the heavy lifting in their multi-million-dollar transaction.

Big fucking mistake.

Now he was completely drained, and his body was determined to go to sleep on him right there on the street. His vision was fine, but his motor skills seemed to have abandoned him. He reached the glass doors of his apartment building lobby, leaning a little too heavily against the glass. Fishing around in his pocket for his keycard, he muttered a string of curses when his hand came up empty. He glanced up and rapped his knuckles. Thank God, the guard recognized him and buzzed him inside.

"Mr. Redmond." The security guard nodded, a knowing smile on the older man's lips.

"Hey, Randy," he greeted, wincing at the slur of his words.

A few more steps and he reached the elevator. After much effort focusing on the series of floor buttons on the panel, he pressed the button to the fifteenth floor and it lit up. He leaned his head back on the mirrored walls, resting. Jesus, it was like he was drunk, but he knew it was sheer exhaustion.

It had been a hell of a day. After two months of negotiations, sleepless nights, long hours, and no chance of reviving his obsolete social life, he'd closed the massive real estate deal, and closed it earlier than he'd anticipated. Everyone demanded they go out and celebrate. He just wanted to crash and sleep off all of the stress pent up inside him.

He was going to walk into his bedroom and face-plant on his bed and not move all weekend from that spot.

Tanner would be out with his girlfriend, Layla, celebrating. It was Halloween, wasn't it? A little grin tugged at his lips. The apartment would be empty and *quiet*. The perfect benefit of arriving home early. He'd told Tanner he wouldn't be back until Sunday, and it was only Friday now. He expected his little brother and girlfriend would be out partying the night away, giving him total silence and a soft bed to crash on without any disturbances.

The second the elevator doors slid open with a soft hiss, he heard the music and the erratic noises of a party. Laughter, voices, all coming from their apartment.

Fucking hell.

"Tanner," he growled, fists clenched.

So the partying tonight was *in*, not *out*.

Jared contemplated turning around and finding a hotel, or worse, calling Shana. No, bad idea. They'd dated on and off during law school and after, but they'd never been exclusive. Currently he and Shana were off. *Definitely off.*

Lousy timing for Tanner to throw a damn party.

That was the main problem with letting his twenty-four-year-old brother live with him. He'd thought it would be nice to spend some time with his little brother, but with his work schedule he barely saw Tanner. The one night they might have hung out, he was too tired to care. He was not in the mood to dodge drunken graduate students all night and try to drown out all the racket they were making. Luck wasn't with him tonight. Fuck, he was turning into a crotchety old man if he was going to let a party piss him off.

The door to their place was unlocked, and when he swung the door open, a wave of fresh sound engulfed him. His eardrums throbbed, and he winced at the explosion of the music that drilled into his skull like nails. Scantily-dressed girls bounced about to the pounding rhythm of the music along with guys who were watching with giddy-schoolboy expressions. Some of them cheered and smiled, drunkenly overjoyed that a new person had shown up to the party. Several familiar faces, Tanner's friends, waved at him or nodded as he walked past them.

"Jared! I thought you weren't coming home till tomorrow?" A zombie stripper stepped in front of him, hands on her hips. Through the gory makeup he thought he recognized her.

"Layla?"

Tanner's girlfriend was dressed as a zombie stripper. Only Layla could manage to pull off that look.

"Layla, what the hell is going on?" he demanded, gesturing to the insanity. A girl in a sexy *Lara Croft* costume was singing a bad karaoke cover of "Somebody's Watching Me." Holy fuck. He was going to need some noise-cancelling headphones to survive this shit. For a brief second he considered tossing everyone out on their damn asses, but this place was half Tanner's and he'd told Tanner he wouldn't be here tonight. Brother code demanded he suffer through this bullshit.

Layla didn't look chagrined in the least. "It's Halloween. Oh, and Felicity's birthday, obviously."

"Who is Felicity?" He'd never met anyone named Felicity. Not that it was surprising, because he was never around when his brother was hanging out with Layla and their friends. He didn't really remember what it was like to be that carefree. Law school and work had a way of consuming a person's good memories.

"Scratch that, I don't care. Is this thing"—he waved a hand around—"ending anytime soon?" He shifted his briefcase strap over his shoulder. His suit was starting to suffocate him, and as much as he liked the particular steel-gray tie he wore at the moment, he was desperate enough to cut it right off his neck if he couldn't get to his room fast enough.

"Uh..." She licked her lips. "Don't know. But you said you weren't coming back until Sunday."

"Well, here I am and tired as fuck. So I'm going to bed. Try to keep it down," he growled.

"Uh, Jared." She dodged around him, trying to prevent him from getting past her.

"What did you do?" He arched a brow, sensing by the way her eyes widened and she shifted in her stilettos that something was wrong.

"I might have given your bed away." Layla bit her lip, yet she was brave enough to still meet his eyes.

"What do you mean you gave my bed away?"

She attempted to smile. "You were *supposed* to be gone until Sunday, and Felicity needed a place to stay tonight. It's late, and I didn't want her to go home alone. She lives in a sketchy part of town—so I told her she could crash in your bed since *you* weren't going to be here." She glared at him, accusing him of something he wasn't entirely sure was his fault. "So she's in your room tonight." She ended with a finality that did not entirely make sense to his tired brain.

"Let me get this straight. Some girl is in my bed... right now?"

Layla swallowed, her eyes darting away before coming back to him. "Um...yeah?"

"No," he stated and stalked toward his room, Layla at his heels. Whoever this Felicity person was, she was in his bed, and since it was *his* bed, whatever Layla and this girl had seemed to think otherwise, he'd have her out of it.

Reaching his bedroom door, he crashed it open and strode in, prepared for all the hell and fury that came with drunk, twenty-something females—and instead, as his eyes adjusted, he found a princess in his bed.

Layla clattered behind on her too-tall stilettos. "Jared, wait—"

He pushed the door open, and a yellow beam of light from the hallway cut across the dark room, revealing a figure lying across his bed.

A princess. There was a princess in his bed.

The burgundy-and-gold gown was draped over his comforter with pearls glowing like tiny moons on the bodice of her gown.

What the fuck?

"Please don't wake her," Layla begged.

Wake her? Jared shook his head. *What nonsense.* He wasn't a romantic. Even though she was certainly a fantasy. All luscious curves and mystery. Her dark auburn hair cascading over the pillow looked soft. His hands ached to reach out and fist in the strands. She looked like the kind of woman a young man dreamed about and ruined his sheets over, the kind of woman he'd stopped dreaming about a long time ago because he was convinced they didn't exist.

He didn't turn to look at Layla as he spoke. "Who is that?"

"Felicity Hart. Birthday girl and, more importantly, my best friend." The threat was heavily implied. Don't screw with Layla or her friends. Her loyalty in that respect was one of the things he admired most about his brother's girlfriend.

Layla's fingers curled around his biceps and squeezed, getting his attention.

"I told her she could sleep in your room since you weren't supposed to be here. It's the only place available for her to sleep."

"I'm not giving up *my* bed. I worked seventy hours this week. I'm going to sleep." He got one step inside his room before Layla practically tackled him, climbing up his back like a spider monkey.

"You. Will. Not. Wake. Her. Up," Layla growled, nails digging into his arms. "She has a really important research paper due tomorrow, and she needs to sleep."

"She can stay, but I'm sharing my bed with her. End of discussion. Go back to your party." With a little shove, he made sure Layla couldn't get back in before he shut the door in her face.

When he turned back around, he studied the girl in his bed. Without the hallway light he could barely make out her features. Just a silhouette, really, of a princess. Arousal slammed into him. He felt like an idiot. He never dated anyone who was still in school. They were too young. A year ago he'd tried to date a girl who was twenty-four, but she'd gotten pissed every time he'd had to work late. She didn't get the pressures of his job. None of the girls younger than him seemed to understand that. Layla was all right, but she was still a kid. He needed someone mature who was at the same point in her life as him, an adult.

The hot little princess was the last thing he needed to be thinking about.

Don't think about her or how much fun it would be to wake her up and kiss her. Just be a gentleman and go to bed.

His inner voice was a goddamn control freak, but he was thankful someone was still responsible.

Turning away, he started to strip out of his work clothes. He kicked his shoes off and then slipped a pair of pajama bottoms on. He didn't bother with a shirt. He always got a little hot at night anyway. As he moved deeper into the room, he caught his foot on a chair. It screeched as it slid across the wood, and he winced, catching himself against the back of it. He glanced at the bed, but the girl hadn't woken. A few quick steps and then he hit the bed, landing on his stomach and bouncing a little. The princess next to him didn't stir. He shifted a couple of inches and slid one arm beneath his pillow to puff it up as he laid his head down. The toll of the night's celebrations dragged him to the edge of the abyss of sleep. He was so close...

A little gasp and a half-strangled whimper pulled him to the surface again. "Whah?" He groaned and rolled onto his side facing the girl.

She was thrashing and whimpering beside him. Her hands clawed at the bodice of her dress, as though trying to escape it.

"Damn it!" He sat up and flicked on the lamp by his side of the bed. The wash of color in the room showed how flushed the girl was. She still shifted and kicked, moaning as if in pain. Jared leaned over and gently jostled her shoulder.

"Hey, kid, wake up."

She jolted awake. Bright gray eyes like liquid mercury flashed in shock and fear as her gaze fell on him.

"Hi," he said.

The princess blinked, her eyes darting around the room, then back to him, focusing on his bare chest. Her pupils dilated.

"Did we...um...who—" She shook her head as though to clear it. "Who are you, and what are you doing here?"

Jared let out a raspy chuckle. "I'm the one who should be asking questions. But it's been a long day and I'm beat. I'm Jared, and you are in *my* bed."

He stood and walked back to his cherrywood dresser. His fingers curled around the brass handle, and he opened the top drawer.

"You're Tanner's brother?" Her voice was soft, husky. It rolled over him, soothing his irritation.

He selected a silk striped button-down nightshirt and a pair of boxers from his drawer and then returned to the bed. "Here." He held the clothes out to her.

"What are those for?" she asked. One elegant brow rose.

"You. You woke up clawing at your dress. Looks like it's too tight around your chest and it's restricting your breathing. Unless you have clothes of your own, you're changing into these so we can both get some sleep. Layla said you had some paper due tomorrow."

When she opened her mouth, he could see the protest in her eyes and it amused him. *Feisty little thing.* And damned if he didn't picture all the things he'd like to do to that little mouth.

"Take the clothes and change in the bathroom. *Now.*" He deepened his voice, and she hopped out of bed, snatching the clothes as she darted into the bathroom. She froze, then slowly looked over her shoulder at him.

"What?"

"My dress...it's the laces in the back. I can't reach them."

A sigh escaped him. "Come here." He crooked a finger and sat farther back on his bed. She sidled up to him, bashfulness in her every movement.

There was something sinful and suggestive about the way she nibbled her bottom lip. He twirled a finger, indicating for her to spin around. She offered her back to him. The silk ribbons on the back of her gown came undone easily enough, but he was surprised to see the second set of laces beneath, which belonged to a corset. It was black with embroidered red roses that set off the color of the loose tangles of her hair. The strands teased the back of his hands as he unlaced the corset. The creamy skin of her lower back made his mouth go dry. The princess was trying to kill him with these temptations.

All too soon the view disappeared as she rushed into the adjoining bathroom to change.

He fell back onto the bed, staring up at the ceiling. His fingers tapped a rhythm on his stomach as he waited. This was not at all how he'd predicted his night would go. He wasn't complaining—not exactly.

The princess emerged, gown gone. She looked so young, standing there dwarfed in his button-down shirt and a hint of his boxers beneath the hem at her mid-thighs. Her gorgeous hair was wild and long, and it looked like she'd been well loved in bed. He didn't miss the swell of her full breasts against the thin, expensive silk. The top button was low down her chest, exposing a wealth of creamy skin. Damn.

He was about to say something bad, something that his exhausted mind would probably get him slapped for, when his bedroom door burst open and light from the hallway illuminated them both.

"Dude...found a bed." A man wearing the bottom half of a stormtrooper costume stumbled toward Jared's bed. Behind him trailed a girl in a Playboy Bunny outfit.

Jared glanced at Felicity, who'd frozen in shock, her hands pulling the button-up shirt closed against her throat, her cheeks a bright pink in the dim light.

"Oh...hey..." The stormtrooper finally noticed Jared as Jared got to his feet, scowling. "Do you mind if we—"

"Get the fucking hell out of my room," Jared growled. "*Now.*" He may have been almost half-dead with fatigue, but he could still throw a punch if he needed to.

"But come on, man, I want to get laid..." the boy whispered too loudly, and the bunny behind him giggled.

"I'll lay you flat on your goddamn ass if you don't get lost." Jared took a menacing step toward the inebriated pair, and they stumbled back into the hall. Jared didn't hesitate. He slammed his bedroom door in the wooden frame and clicked the lock into place before he turned back to face Felicity. Her hand was covering her mouth, and her eyes were wide.

"Sorry about that, princess. I locked the door. No one else will stumble in—I promise."

She blinked, dropped her hand, and then her eyes drifted from the door to his face as though debating whether she was safe with him in a locked room.

"Come on. I don't bite." *Hard,* he silently added, and flashed what he knew was a wolfish grin.

"I could sleep elsewhere," she hedged, playing with the collar of the button-down shirt. "Layla said you'd be gone all weekend."

"It's fine. This thing is a California king. Plenty of room for both of us. It's just one night."

He waited for her to pad on little bare feet to her side of the bed. It dipped slightly as she got in under the covers. She tensed when he crawled beneath the blankets, but after a moment, when he didn't move toward her, she blew out a breath. He rolled away to turn off the lamp by his bedside, then settled back, puffing his pillow again as he lay on his back and closed his eyes. A sweet, subtle scent filled his nose, like vanilla and fresh rain. When the princess shifted, trying to get comfortable, the scent grew stronger. Her scent.

"Thanks for letting me stay. I'm Felicity, by the way."

He could hear the yawn in her voice, and it made him grin.

"Good night, princess," he murmured.

She didn't respond. The soft little sound of her faint breaths did something funny to his chest. It tightened, and he sucked in a deep breath, hoping to ease the tension.

Now was not the time to be having a soft spot for a woman. He had so much to worry about at work, especially with Shana and her father. There wasn't time to seduce a sweet little princess, even if he wanted to. She really was a cute little thing, though.

Not for me. He sighed and let his body crash.

CHAPTER 2

The cell phone alarm buzzed, a light musical chime accompanying the vibrations. Felicity fumbled on the nightstand for the phone and silenced it.

6:00 a.m. Two and a half hours until her American Colonial Art paper was due. The urge to get up and get moving just wasn't there. The bed was warm, and she felt safe. The last thing she wanted to do was get up and think about a bunch of colonists and loyalists duking it out in the seventeen hundreds and how that had affected painting styles in Colonial America. Right now she wanted to stay where she was, cocooned in heat, and drift back to that pleasant place between being awake and dreaming.

It was then she noticed the long, muscled arm

curled around her waist, tucking her back against a hard, warm body.

What the—

Another rattling buzz. This time it came from the other side of the bed. She rolled over, careful not to wake the man in bed next to her. A wall of muscled male chest met her face. Her gaze raked up the bare torso of the man to his face where it rested on his pillow.

Jared Redmond.

She was sharing a bed with Tanner's brother. Had she really let him untie her dress and corset last night? Her eyes closed for a brief instant as she pushed back her shyness. He was still asleep, and she took advantage of it to study his face. It was a nice face, not too handsome, yet somehow sexy and incredibly attractive. Strong jaw, aquiline nose, too-long dark eyelashes fanned over slightly tanned skin. Dark brows winged over eyes that she knew had to be dark brown like his brother's. He was the sort of man who wasn't a pretty boy, yet he had some serious animal magnetism even while he slept.

Her fingers tingled as she resisted the urge to reach out and trace his lips. The bottom lip was slightly fuller than the top. His hair was a rich chocolate, long enough to tunnel her fingers through. Would it be silky or slightly rough in texture? She nibbled her bottom lip.

This was the closest she'd ever been to a man before —at least in bed—and it was fascinating and a little unnerving. A shadow of a beard made him look older, a little rugged. The pit of her stomach dropped, and she shivered with excitement. He was only thirty, but that felt so much older than her at the moment. He was a man.

Jared had the body of a man, unlike the graduate student guys in her classes. He was hot and dangerous looking, and every time she thought about that, her stomach quivered. She was in *his* bed, as he'd said the night before. She'd been helpless to resist when he'd gently commanded her to undress with that deep baritone voice of his. She glanced down at herself. His shirt and boxers were large and comfortable on her, and the intimacy of wearing his clothes had her heart thrumming like a hummingbird's wings.

That other phone was buzzing again on his side of the bed. Suddenly he jerked, rolling away as he picked up the phone.

Had he been awake this whole time? Did he know she'd been just staring at him? Had he meant to be holding her so close when she'd woken up?

God, I'm such an idiot.

"Hell," Jared muttered and fell back on his bed, eyes closed, his phone silenced. Two breaths more, and then he spoke again. "So you getting up? I'll let you shower first."

"What?" He was offering her his shower? Before she wouldn't have thought twice about using it, but now that its owner was here, she'd figured she'd skip it until after her test. The idea of her being naked with just a door between them sent a little shiver through her.

"The shower. It's yours. I'm still waking up." He twisted to face her, propping his head on his hand to stare at her.

"Get moving, princess. Or else I might give in to my desire to kiss you. A man can only stand so much temptation." He chuckled.

Felicity shot out of the bed like she'd been fired out of a cannon. Kiss her? Was he serious?

"I'm a good kisser," he called out after her.

He was still laughing, probably because of the look she knew he must be seeing on her face. His grin hit her right behind the knees. She retreated, her back hitting his dresser.

"I...um...have a term paper due." That was stupid. She was making it worse by opening her mouth. She mentally smacked herself and ran to the shower. Cranking the nozzle to hot, she picked up her bag from the bathroom floor and searched for her toiletries.

The water burned her skin, and she sighed. Her own apartment had hot water only when the water heater thought it could handle the building's demands, which wasn't often. And when it did bother to work, the pipes rocked inside the walls, creating a banging noise that drove her crazy.

Staying here at Jared's apartment was like staying in a four-star hotel. Scrubbing her face in her hands, she let the water pour over her. The tension in her shoulders eased. Not once last night had she woken up. Where she'd grown up, she'd fallen asleep to the melody of crickets and other country sounds. But here in Chicago, with her apartment's paper-thin walls, all she heard were the violent sounds of the city outside. Ambulances, shouting neighbors, banging pipes, slamming stairwell doors, and the endless creaks and groans as the elevator ground through its gears. Felicity was lucky to get even an hour or two of uninterrupted sleep. Last night had been amazing. Just silence and warmth. Ironically, sleeping with a total stranger—and a man, at that—had been one of the most restful nights of sleep she'd had in a long time.

Felicity's skin tingled as she remembered the way it felt to roll over and see him so close. Shock aside, it had been nice. Layla must *never* find out. She'd try to hook her up with Jared. It would be a bad idea. Between school and work, she didn't have time. Not to mention she and Jared were nothing alike and had nothing in common. He was a hotshot lawyer, and she was an art student. She doubted he'd even be interested in her, his jokes about kisses aside.

Rinsing the last bit of soap and conditioner away, she slipped out of the shower and pulled one of the large fluffy white towels off the shelf next to the shower. The towel fit around her body perfectly, and she was able to tuck the corner of it in near the tops of her breasts to keep it on so she could rummage around the drawers of the bathroom counter. There had to be a hairdryer in here somewhere. She hadn't thought to pack one since Layla had said she could borrow one, but it wasn't as though she could go parading past Jared in nothing but a towel to find Layla's hairdryer.

"What do you need?"

Jared's deep voice made her freeze as she bent over the drawer, her bottom in the air.

"I can help you find whatever you need...although I do love this angle, if you want to keep looking for whatever it is."

"Oh!" She whirled around, hands clutching her towel so it wouldn't drop.

When she raised her gaze, she found him standing in the open bathroom door, wearing only pajama pants. He leaned one shoulder against the doorjamb. His body was lightly tan, the muscles lean but impressive now that she could see them at a better angle. His pants hung on his narrow hips, and she gulped at the visible

V-shaped line of muscles at his hips that seemed to point farther south to places hidden from her eyes. A perfect six-pack. How did a guy get those? They looked too good to be true. She certainly didn't look like she lived in the gym. Her fingers went white-knuckled on the towel. The last thing she wanted was for him to see her fuller figure. No matter how many diets she tried or how much she exercised, she could never get down to anything below a size twelve.

"What are you looking for?" he asked again. His gaze lazily drifted from her face down the length of her body. Was that approval in his eyes? Why did she suddenly want him to approve of her?

"I...uh...hairdryer, please?" She was usually more articulate. The man had the ability to destroy her control over her own mouth.

He pointed to below the sink. "Should be there."

"Thanks."

"Coffee or tea?" he asked.

"Tea," she replied without thinking.

"I'll make some in the kitchen. Come out when you're done." He didn't give her a chance to protest. The bathroom door closed, and he was gone.

Felicity scrambled through her morning routine, and in fifteen minutes she was dressed in jeans and a comfortable navy-blue sweater with a gray anchor on it. Sitting back on Jared's bed, she tugged on her worn pair of leather ankle boots. The bedroom was empty, so she headed to the kitchen. A few lone plastic cups lay on surfaces around the apartment, the only remnants of the wild party from the night before. Other than that, the place was surprisingly clean. Out of habit, she collected the few cups and walked into the kitchen to throw them away.

"Over here, sailor." Jared was at the other end of the kitchen, where the table was set for two.

He looked more delicious than the breakfast he'd prepared. He stood there in his pajama pants and shirtless, making her mouth water. His feet were bare, and for some reason that made her smile. She tried not to look at his chest, but it was pretty hard not to admire its muscled perfection. It reminded her of the times she and Layla would spend a night eating pizza and drooling over the gorgeous hunks in *Men's Health* magazine. Jared could have been posing for an article on six-pack abs.

Even though he was the one half-dressed, it made her feel strangely naked. The half-smile that hovered around his lips told her he knew she was uncomfortable and a little flushed.

Waffles, scrambled eggs, and bacon were already on the plates, and two cups of tea were waiting, steam coiling up in the air in milky tendrils. Her mind blanked. He was feeding her, too? What sort of man did that? Take care of a woman? Definitely none she knew. He fed her, clothed her...without threats, without demanding she accept what he offered. Something about that made her chest ache. She needed to regain control of her emotions.

"Sailor?" she asked.

"Your sweater." His lips twitched as he sat down at the table.

She glanced down at the anchor. "Oh, right." What was with him and the nicknames? Kid, princess, sailor...

She dropped into the seat across from him and reached for her cup of tea. The porcelain cup burned her fingers—not quite to the point of pain, but enough to make the rest of her warm. She loved that about tea, the way even holding it in her hands could erase a bone-deep chill.

Jared watched her. The weight of his gaze was an almost tangible touch. Felicity shifted in her chair as she wriggled under his scrutiny.

"What paper do you have this morning?" he asked after a moment of painfully awkward silence.

"It's an analysis of the changing artistic painting styles in Colonial America during the Revolutionary War." She sipped her tea. Irish Breakfast. Her favorite.

Jared dug into his waffle, chewing thoughtfully. "You pick that by choice or force?"

She didn't understand his question. "I picked it. I'm an art history major."

"Ah...that explains the costume. You, princess, are a nerd." His judgmental smirk made her want to punch him, yet she still also found it infuriatingly attractive.

A prickle of indignation buried beneath her skin. *Nerd? Nerd!*

"I am *not*. Appreciating history isn't bad," she countered.

With a scrape of a fork over the plate he continued to eat, his whiskey brown eyes fixed on her every few seconds.

"Never said it was bad."

Okay. Felicity wasn't sure how to respond to that, so she decided to eat in silence. After a few bites—delicious ones—she realized she had relaxed a little more around him. She'd slept with Jared. Well, not *slept* with him, but being around him and not making a fool of herself by being too awkward was impressive when she'd rarely spent time alone with any guys back home. Instead, her heart beat a little quicker, her mouth was desert-dry, and her hands trembled with excitement.

"So...Layla said you're an attorney?" She decided to try small talk again. Her plate was wiped clean and so was his. He leaned back in his chair and put his hands behind his head, fingers laced as he studied her.

"Yeah. I focus on real estate transactions. I'm an associate attorney at Pimms & Associates LLP."

The name didn't sound familiar, not that it should have. She and Jared moved in very different circles. She was a graduate student with no connections to any big companies in the city, especially not law firms. And she wasn't from Omaha like Jared. She was just a small-town girl, but he didn't make her feel that way.

For the last couple of months of being around Tanner, she'd learned the Redmonds were wealthy, but they had earned it through hard work. More than once Layla had confessed it was one of the things she loved about Tanner. He wasn't a spoiled playboy. He played hard, sure, but he worked hard, too. He was an engineering major. Those students had an intense curriculum. Felicity and Layla joked that one look at Tanner's textbooks gave them headaches.

"Want another waffle?" Jared's voice cut through her thoughts. He was standing right beside her. *When had he moved?*

"No thanks." She patted her stomach. "Quite full."

"Okay. Just make sure you eat enough to fuel your brain for your research paper." He ruffled a hand over her hair, messing up the artful windblown look she'd spent several minutes that morning perfecting.

"Hey!" she said, swatting his hand away. When he

caught her hand and tugged her body against his, she closed her eyes, praying for a kiss.

Gentle fingers cupped her chin and lifted her face. "Look at me, princess."

She pried one eye open, her heart beating wildly. To her surprise, Jared was studying her, but only kindness and curiosity shone in his warm brown eyes. Like rich maple syrup... She blinked.

"There you are," he murmured more to himself than to her. "Welcome back." He grinned and patted her cheek.

She couldn't escape the crushing disappointment. Why hadn't he kissed her? Was there something wrong with her?

The gesture was patronizing, yet Felicity couldn't summon any anger. No one had ever been playful with her or treated her like a kid, or maybe like a sister. But the look in his eyes—there was something dark and wild there, something that did funny things to her insides. Her lips pursed in a tight line.

"Don't frown, princess." He laughed, his back still to her.

She shot him a scathing look, hot enough to melt steel.

He was already walking back to the sink, whistling a tune under his breath.

"Better get going if you're going to make it to your

class." He joined her back at the table and held out a wad of cash. "Cab money." He set the money in her hand and then walked back to the sink, apparently oblivious to her standing there gaping. The water ran as he scrubbed pots. A lawyer who did his own dishes? What next?

"I have money." She attempted to put the money on the counter next to him, but he caught her wrist. The warmth of his hand, slightly slick with dish soap, made her heart skip a beat. She met his gaze, steel determination forcing her not to mentally cower.

"Consider it an apology for whatever I may have said or done last night and for disrupting your sleep. I really wasn't supposed to come back last night, but we closed our sale on time without any issues, so I was able to come back early."

Apology? Was he serious? He'd saved her from a drunken stormtrooper and a Playboy Bunny. She'd felt completely safe with him, like she had her very own knight in shining armor guarding her while she slept. That wasn't the sort of thing a girl like her would forget. She'd never been the damsel-in-distress type, but she had to admit she liked knowing someone had her back, that she wasn't alone. But it wasn't meant to be. She was hoping her boss at her art gallery was going to give her a personal recommendation for a position at the Los Angeles County Museum of Art, or LACMA as it was called. If she got that job, she'd be leaving Chicago at the end of the school year when she graduated. That meant no dating, no love—not here, not with him.

"Look, this is really—" She pulled out of his grasp, unnerved by how unafraid of his touch she was.

"Let a man be chivalrous once in a while. We like it. Makes us feel needed." He dried his hands off and tucked the money in the front of her jeans.

Heat exploded through her in an almost violent rush as he invaded her space yet again. Why was she letting him affect her like that?

"No argument?" he teased.

She shook her head, her mind a little blank as she got lost in the splinters of gold and the flecks of green in his eyes. She hadn't seen that before. They weren't hazel, but the brown had a myriad of subtle colors in it. His eyes made her think of summer sun and lazy afternoons, the few in her life she'd been able to enjoy. She licked her lips, trying to erase the cotton-dry feeling in her mouth.

"Go get your stuff and get out of here. I don't want you to miss out on the colonial artwork." He winked.

Felicity finally found control of her body, and she hastily left the kitchen to pack her things. She left her change of clothes in her gym bag in Jared's room, even though she wanted to leave it with Layla. There was no way she was interrupting Layla and Tanner in bed.

Right now she had to focus on her term paper. She couldn't afford to jeopardize her scholarship. Not even to linger one more minute in the presence of a handsome man who was just a little too sexy and a little too dangerous. Not scary dangerous, but the sort of dangerous that, if she wasn't careful, she might fall hopelessly in love with him. She'd had her heart broken already, and trust wasn't easy for her. The last thing she needed was Jared destroying her carefully-constructed fortress.

Yeah, he was dangerous all right.

CHAPTER 3

Felicity haunted his thoughts. A flicker of light against the windows reminded him of her flashing gray eyes. God, she was something else. Jared grinned. It had been a long time since he'd had so much fun teasing a girl. The look on her face when he'd tucked the cab money back in her pocket—she'd been all flushed and wide-eyed. *Damn.* He'd gotten hard as a rock imagining how else he could have made her all pink and hot. But she was young. A graduate student.

So why did he keep reliving last night like some teenager in a fantasy? There was more to it than a warm body in bed beside him. It was the way she'd fallen asleep almost instantly, showing complete trust. Sharing a bed for the night with another person was more intimate than sex. You let your guard down, had no ready defenses. Most people refused to let themselves become that vulnerable. He was one of them.

But last night, he could have stayed next to her forever. The sweet smell of her, the rhythm of her light breathing, and the way she'd curled up against him until just before dawn. Jared doubted she remembered that part of the night. He'd have to remind her later, just to see a blush creep across her cheeks.

There couldn't be a later, though.

Suddenly gripped by a bad mood, he stalked down the hall to his bedroom. Even though he kept his windows fairly tinted against the sun, the bold rays lit up the room. A streak of gold and burgundy caught his eye.

A wolfish grin tugged his lips back up.

The princess had left her gown.

Walking over to his bed, he reached out and touched the silk, which gleamed in the light. A hint of heat from the sun warmed his fingers as he picked up the gown. His eyes closed as he remembered the way she'd offered her back to him, so shy and yet completely trusting him. His hands tangling in the laces as he sought to undo them. The whisper of silk against skin.

Arousal slammed into him. His eyes flew open, and he forced himself to let go of the gown. Since when had he become so sentimental?

"Morning, Jared," Layla greeted him from his doorway, dressed in Tanner's shirt and boxers. Her long dark hair was sexy and rumpled. No doubt she and Tanner had partied well into the night.

"Layla," he answered and shifted slightly to block the view of Felicity's gown on his bed.

Her eyes tracked the movement like a cat sensing the darting shadow of a mouse.

"What's that?" She was instantly alert as she padded across his room.

"Nothing," he growled, taking a step toward her. Layla had no sense of boundaries, the result of too many siblings growing up, he supposed.

"Oh yeah? Sure doesn't look like nothing." She winkled her nose as she giggled. Then without warning, she dove around him and snatched up the gown. "This is Felicity's costume. Why do you have it?"

Jared licked his lips. It never ceased to amaze him how she could intimidate him, despite her small size. He stood nearly a foot taller than her, but when she got that look in her eyes, it made even him want to retreat.

"She left it here when she took off for her class." He attempted to wrestle the dress back from Layla's hands, but the young woman kept a possessive grip on the fabric, and he didn't want to tear it.

"Uh-huh." She didn't sound all that convinced. "I'll just take this, if you don't mind. It's not like you need it."

With a saucy little wink she started for the door, then stopped to look over her shoulder. "Oh, Jared, how was last night, by the way?" She paused in the doorway, her gaze on him assessing.

"Fine." That was all she was going to get.

He waited until Layla had disappeared before he shut the door and headed for the shower. Technically, he didn't have to work today. The sale for their client, the buyer, had gone through yesterday. After this sale, things at the office would settle down. At least for a few days.

Jared cranked the shower nozzle on and stripped out of his pajama bottoms. When he stepped inside, a sweet vanilla scent hit him hard. Felicity. Her body wash? Or maybe her shampoo? He reached for his own shampoo, a minty-scented bottle. Disappointment prickled inside him at the way the spearmint covered the vanilla. One more trace of last night's encounter was gone. With a frustrated growl, he scrubbed his scalp, lathering the shampoo into a thick froth before he rinsed.

A whole day. He had a whole day to burn and do whatever he wanted. Part of him was tempted to crash on his bed and sleep the rest of the day away. But that would only screw up his sleep schedule. He got so little as it was. It would have been worth it if he could have slept in with Felicity in his arms, although if she was there, he'd likely be tempted to do other things than sleep.

How is Felicity doing on her research? It had been six years since he'd been in college. Seemed more like a hundred. Law school and college were nothing alike. Undergrad had been fun. He'd worked hard and played hard. He didn't know what getting a master's degree was like compared to law school, though. Law school—that was the equivalent of joining the army and, rather than going to boot camp for training, just being dropped into the middle of a war zone with a water gun. He had barely gotten out of that experience alive. If it hadn't been for Shana—and more importantly, her father—he might never have landed his current associate position.

He scowled. These were never thoughts he liked to linger on, the possibility that he'd only been hired because he'd dated a partner's daughter. Yeah, really bruising to his ego.

Jared was tempted to linger in the shower, relishing the way the water soothed his tense muscles. But he couldn't avoid the inevitable. With a heavy sigh, he shut the water off and exited the shower. He reached for a fresh towel and saw the one that Felicity had used dangling over one peg. It was impossible to forget the look on her face when he'd caught her searching his bathroom. The puffy white towel had hugged her full figure, making her look soft and cuddly. He'd been torn between the desire to hug her to him, stripping the towel away to lick the crystalline droplets from her skin, or to just drag her to bed to make love the rest of the day.

His cock twitched in a silent salute at the idea. Damn. He needed to get his mind off the little princess. Princess. She'd left her gown. Surely she'd want it back, right? The pearl-encrusted bodice and silk fabric looked pricey.

It would be rude of him not to return the dress. He had no other plans today. Might be fun to tease her again. Striding over to the chest, he grabbed jeans and a black T-shirt. No suit today, thank God. As much as he loved dressing well, sometimes a man just needed jeans. Once he was dressed, he went in search of Layla and the costume.

His brother's girlfriend was in the kitchen, perched on the counter, bare legs swinging as she texted someone and sipped coffee from one of the black mugs he and Tanner had in their cupboards.

"Where's Felicity's costume?"

She didn't pause in her texting. "My room. Why?"

"I'm not working today, and I'd like to return it to her."

This made Layla's fingers freeze above her phone's screen. Her dark eyes drew a slow line up from her phone to his face. A glint of mischief peeked out from beneath her lashes.

"Mmmkay. Do you need her phone number and address? I wouldn't call for at least an hour. She has to finish the paper and turn it in to the professor around eleven a.m."

"Good point." He pulled his phone out of his pocket and waited for Layla to give him Felicity's info. When she was done, he pocketed the phone and returned to his room. He unloaded his briefcase on his desk and happily turned his mind off work, an event that rarely happened.

"You should take her bag, too." Layla was in his doorway again, pointing to the blue gym bag half-hidden behind his door. He'd missed that somehow. Layla hadn't.

"Okay. Thanks." He retrieved the bag and set it on his bed.

"So what happened last night?" Layla asked, her tone neutral as she walked over to his bed and plopped down on it like she owned the place.

"Kid, it's none of your business."

She kicked one leg off his bed, grinning like a Cheshire cat. "She's my best friend. It's definitely my business."

"You only met her like a few months ago, right?" He

wanted to know more about his bed partner, but he didn't want Layla getting any crazy ideas in her head.

"Sometimes how long you've known a person doesn't matter." Layla fixed him with a catlike gaze full of intentions he couldn't read clearly. "She and I just clicked."

He understood that. Sometimes you met someone and they just fit into place, like an intricate puzzle. You fit, no questions, no doubts. Something about Felicity made him feel like that. He'd never felt that way about a girl before, and frankly, it was a little unnerving.

"If you like her, Jared, be careful. You break her heart, I break your balls." Layla mimicked a karate chop motion.

He chuckled. "You don't need to worry. She's sweet but way too young for me. I just feel like I owe her after last night. I should have taken the couch."

Layla bit her bottom lip but didn't bother him further. "Uh-huh." She slid off his bed and walked to the door, only pausing once to motion with two fingers pointing at her eyes, then to his face. She would be watching him.

He grinned and picked up his phone and Felicity's things. He wanted to be ready the moment she turned her paper in. He thought about surprising her. Would that be weird? To show up at her place? No, it wasn't like he was some creep. He was just giving her bag back.

With a tenderness that shocked even himself, he folded her gown and then tucked it into her bag. A flash of bright red caught his attention deep in the bag. Using his finger, he extricated the item.

Red silk panties. Not a thong, just a normal pair, but the way the silk caught the light and slid smoothly against his skin... God, was the girl determined to drive him insane with lust?

"Damn it." Guilt nipped at his insides as he tucked the red silk underwear back into the bag. He checked his watch again. Half an hour to go before he could text her. Excitement jittered inside him, a strange feeling he hadn't felt in a long time. He couldn't wait to see his princess again, make her blush again, make her smile.

At a quarter till eleven, Felicity printed off the last page of her term paper from the library computer system and hastily stapled it and her resource list as well as her painting examples to the back. Then she slipped it into a clean, crisp black binder.

She was done. The relief of finishing such an intense research project was immense. She'd been working on this paper for two months, and now she could start on something new for next semester. Felicity left the library and headed toward the classroom building across the narrow sidewalk, tugging her coat up to keep out the cold wind. Her professor always preferred to collect term papers in person in his classroom rather than at his office. She had a sneaking suspicion he enjoyed heightening the tension by making everyone wait in line to hand it to him.

When she arrived at the classroom, a group of students were standing in a small circle showing their papers to each other and muttering as they examined each other's work. Felicity wasn't going to let herself get dragged into that potential drama and let them make her second-guess herself. So she stepped up to the front of the line, her binder ready.

Eyes locked on her as she walked up to Professor Willoughby to hand him her term paper. The middle-aged man leaned back in his chair, feet propped on one corner of the teacher's desk at the front of the classroom.

He was fine-boned, with a rather unremarkable face, except for the way his sudden grins seemed a touch sarcastic. His eyes were always assessing everything around him and reflected back on her with a cleverness that often matched his words. His lectures were actually fun. He cracked historical jokes with a straight face, and only she and a few others seemed to realize that not everything he said was true. Not everyone had figured Professor Willoughby out, but Felicity was pretty sure she had.

"You're sure it's ready?" he challenged, a little smile hovering about his mouth, making the faint laugh lines in his cheeks reveal themselves temporarily.

"Yes. I think I'm okay." She smiled. He was always trying to tease the students and keep them on their toes, but she felt confident of her research. As she left the class, she could almost hear her professor's silent laughter.

Halfway out of the classroom building, her cell phone vibrated. She paused, dug the phone out of her pocket, and checked it.

One new message.

Unknown number: *Hey, princess, you left your gown on my bed.*

Princess? It had to be Jared. How in the heck...? *Layla.* She growled. Her best friend had betrayed her. Wasn't that against the girl code? No giving of one's number without permission. Layla was in serious trouble, but she'd deal with her later.

What was she going to do now? Text him back? What could she say? God, she wished she'd done this whole "interact with the male species" before now. If Felicity wasn't so pissed at Layla, she would have texted her and gotten her advice, but that would be such a bad idea to let Layla anywhere near whatever this...thing was between her and Jared.

Her fingers hesitated above the screen. Why was he texting her, anyway? Layla could have easily gotten her dress back to her.

Unknown number: *Don't get shy on me now, princess. We did SLEEP together.*

She saved his number to her contacts and typed a reply.

Felicity: *Is this always going to come up between us?*

Jared: *You didn't just say that, did you? There are lots of things that can come up between us.*

Felicity: *I can't believe you just texted that!*

Jared: *HAHA. I can't believe your mind went there, princess.*

Laughter bubbled up from her, and she couldn't contain it, nor did she want to.

Felicity: *Is Layla still at your apartment?*

Jared: *Yeah...why?*

Felicity: *Tell her she's dead. I'm gonna kill her for giving you my number.*

Jared: *Haha. Will do. Did you get your paper turned in?*

She paused. Her heart skipped a few beats, then rushed to catch up. He wanted to know how her day was? A guy like him was taking time out of his day to ask her if she got her paper completed?

Felicity: *It was good, I think. My research and asser- tions were well thought out.*

Jared: *I'm sure you nailed it.*

The text made her smile, bite her lip, and then she smiled again. He thought she did great. Just thinking about that made her feel good. She didn't dwell on how pathetic it was that she responded so much to his praise.

Jared: *You're still a nerd, btw.*

The smile on her lips stretched even wider. She would have been offended by anyone else calling her that. But after this morning she could only grin.

Jared: *What? No witty comeback?*

Felicity: *Give a girl time to come up with one.*

She tucked her phone in her jeans pocket and headed toward the street so she could hail a cab. It was too cold to make the long walk back to her place. Jared's money still filled her pocket. She hadn't used it, even though she'd been tempted. Boy, had she been tempted. At the curb, she stepped off a step and raised a hand. One of the many yellow cabs waiting for fares skidded into place in front of her. Climbing in, she settled her backpack on her lap and gave the driver her address.

Her phone buzzed again. Another message.

Jared: *You have lunch plans?*

She rolled her eyes and tapped her phone's keyboard.

Felicity: *Don't you have work or something, Mr. Big Shot Lawyer?*

Jared: *Mr. Big Shot Lawyer. That's your comeback? I gave you plenty of time to think of a good one.*

She snickered and then typed.

Felicity: *Seriously?*

Jared: *Seriously. I'm a lawyer. I'm dead serious. And you didn't answer my question.*

Felicity: *What question?*

Jared: *Do you have lunch plans?*

Why was he asking her that? Did he want her to come over and get her costume during lunch? Probably would be easier for her to do that so he could make it to his own important lawyer lunch or whatever it was lawyers did during lunch.

Jared: *Still waiting...*

Felicity: *No plans. Why?*

Jared: *Good.*

She waited for him to explain. No more texts came through. Disappointment slithered into her, bit by bit. The strange elation she'd experienced during their brief and very odd conversation deflated. It was the first real interaction she'd had with a guy her age—well, close to her age. Jared was a *little* older, but in a good kind of way.

The cab ride was fifteen minutes long, and yet Felicity was so lost in her thoughts that she only noticed they'd stopped when the cabbie tapped his fare machine and coughed loudly. She handed him her money, even though she was tempted to give him Jared's. They were even, though. And she didn't like taking handouts.

As she got out of the cab, she stared at the eyesore of an apartment complex in front of her. The red brick was chipped and crumbling, and the plaster in the halls was peeling. Inside she knew aromas of urine and booze would linger in the halls. The cracked sidewalk leading up to the building was a clear reflection of the tenants inside.

Home sweet home. After leaving Jared and Tanner's apartment, she felt like a mortal returning from a brief night on Mount Olympus. *Back to reality.* Her steps slowed when she reached the elevator. A "Broken" sign was taped to the orange-painted metal doors. Three months and the thing had yet to be fixed. She climbed the three flights of stairs to her floor. The overhead lights flickered, buzzing like enraged bees in a low hum.

A tall figure leaned against the wall next to her door at the end of the hall, his back to her. A pool of shadows formed by the lack of hall lights above him made it impossible to see him clearly.

Crap, that wasn't good. Last week the man who lived two doors down from her had gotten jumped by a guy who'd followed him into his apartment and knocked him out. The man had robbed her neighbor and left him bleeding from a nasty head wound for two hours before someone found him and called the police. Ever since then Felicity had been sleeping with one eye open and her cell phone at the ready.

Please, please don't be here to rob me...

OTHER TITLES BY LAUREN SMITH

Historical

The League of Rogues Series

Wicked Designs

His Wicked Seduction

Her Wicked Proposal

Wicked Rivals

Her Wicked Longing

His Wicked Embrace

The Earl of Pembroke

His Wicked Secret

The Wicked Earls Club

The Earl of Pembroke

The Seduction Series

The Duelist's Seduction

The Rakehell's Seduction

The Rogue's Seduction
The Gentleman's Seduction
The Sins and Scandals Series
An Earl By Any Other Name
A Gentleman Never Surrenders
A Scottish Lord for Christmas
Standalone Stories
Tempted by A Rogue
Bewitching the Earl

Contemporary
Ever After Series
Legally Charming
The Surrender Series
The Gilded Cuff
The Gilded Cage
The Gilded Chain
The Darkest Hour
Her British Stepbrother
Forbidden: Her British Stepbrother
Seduction: Her British Stepbrother
Climax: Her British Stepbrother
Forever Be Mine (Coming soon)

Paranormal
Brothers of Ash and Fire
Grigori

Mikhail

Rurik

The Lost Barinov Dragon (coming soon)

Dark Seductions Series

The Shadows of Stormclyffe Hall

The Love Bites Series

The Bite of Winter

Brotherhood of the Blood Moon Series

Blood Moon on the Rise (coming soon)

Sci-Fi Romance

Cyborg Genesis Series

Across the Stars (coming soon)

ABOUT THE AUTHOR

USA TODAY Bestselling Author Lauren Smith is an Oklahoma attorney by day, who pens adventurous and edgy romance stories by the light of her smart phone flashlight app. She knew she was destined to be a romance writer when she attempted to re-write the entire *Titanic* movie just to save Jack from drowning. Connecting with readers by writing emotionally moving, realistic and sexy romances no matter what time period is her passion. She's won multiple awards in several romance subgenres including: New England Reader's Choice Awards, Greater Detroit BookSeller's Best Awards, and a Semi-Finalist award for the Mary Wollstonecraft Shelley Award.

To connect with Lauren, visit her at:
www.laurensmithbooks.com
lauren@Laurensmithbooks.com

www.ingramcontent.com/pod-product-compliance
Lightning Source LLC
Chambersburg PA
CBHW031417200726

48285CB00017BA/2394